"Diana"—his voice was very tense—"please don't talk...

as if we are never going to see each other again. I want to see you and be with you al—" He stopped before he could say the word "always." Ever since he was a child it had been drummed into him that he would have to marry someone in his own set. Bloodlines were extremely important, but seated next to this vibrant, beautiful young woman he found it difficult to control his strong emotions. He took Diana in his arms.

"You might as well know, Diana, I've fallen in love with you. I want you to be my wife."

She broke away from him. "Chris, isn't this all too sudden?"

Turning from him, she tried to rationalize all that had happened in such a short time. "Chris, I must have time to think. There is so much that needs sorting out in my life."

JOAN WINMILL BROWN, who first gained recognition as an English actress, has most recently received plaudits for her skill as an editor and compiler of Christian anthologies. Her reading audience will be delighted by her latest work in the area of Christian romance novels as she writes from her interesting background.

Another Love

JOAN WINMILL BROWN

HARVEST HOUSE PUBLISHERS
Eugene, Oregon 97402

Other Rhapsody Romance Books:

The Heart That Lingers	*June Masters Bacher*
If Love Be Ours	*Joan Winmill Brown*
With All My Heart	*June Masters Bacher*

ANOTHER LOVE

Chapter One

The ultramodern, luxurious offices of *Celebrity Homes* magazine, on the twenty-fifth floor of one of the soaring skyscrapers in Century City, a Los Angeles suburb, was enveloped with an air of tension. It was deadline day. Too much coffee was being consumed and tempers were frazzled.

Diana Lewis was trying to finish the last page of an article on the Beverly Hills home of one of Hollywood's top stars, but her mind kept wandering. Tonight, at 8 P.M., she would be leaving for two assignments in England and then take a three-week vacation in that country. There was still so much to do before she left, but this article took priority. She willed herself to concentrate and finish the last few sentences.

With a feeling of triumph, Diana ripped the page out of her typewriter, gathered together the rest of the article, and pushed her hair back. Gazing for a moment at the sparkling, panoramic view of Los Angeles, she thought excitedly, "Tomorrow I'll be seeing the skyline of London!"

Diana stretched her lissome body and pushed the long, lustrous blonde hair back from her luminous blue eyes. Standing to her feet, she smoothed the skirt of her white linen tailored suit and adjusted her collar. *Celebrity Homes's* editor, Tom Bartlett, could be heard roaring orders to his secretary down the hall. Hastily Diana left her office in search of him.

"Mr. Bartlett, it's finished," she called out as she came up behind his short, stocky figure.

"What's finished?" he boomed.

"The article on Charlotte Taylor's house."

Diana handed it to him, and with a quick, cursory glance through it he mumbled, "Looks good,

Diana, looks good." Adjusting his horn-rimmed glasses (that had slipped down his nose for the umpteenth time that morning), he asked, "Do you have all the information on your English assignments?"

"Yes, Mr. Bartlett."

"*Do* call me Tom," he said exasperatedly. Somehow Diana could never bring herself to call him by his first name. When she had been interviewed by this crusty gentleman, her first reaction was one of surprise. She had imagined he would be a tall, dignified man—aloof to the trials and tribulations of bringing together a highly successful glossy magazine each month. Instead, Tom Barlett's ruffled appearance and craggy face belied the importance of his position. Diana had thought she would never get over the feeling of intimidation. She had been right. Whenever she was in his presence, she felt like a small child again, standing before the principal. Having worked for almost two years at *Celebrity Homes*, Diana at 26 was still not completely assured in the sophisticated world she moved in. Despite the air of confidence she displayed before her fellow employees, her sensitivity had not allowed her to become used to the idea of being so fortunate in having a job she loved, traveling all over the United States and even other parts of the world— and being the envy of many of her friends.

Now her next assignment would take her into the home of England's leading playwright, Jason Winter, whose Georgian mansion, in the southern part of the country, had been restored to its original grandeur. Nestled in one of the most picturesque parts of Sussex, the photos of the great house had intrigued Diana, and she was anticipating a very interesting visit. She would also be covering a leading interior decorator's apartment in Belgrave Square, London, the heart of English nobility. One of her late mother's friends, Janet Nelson, had invited Diana to stay with her at her elegant Chelsea home.

Diana found the work on the magazine challenging; it satisfied the ambitious streak in her that seemed to constantly propel her toward the necessity for perfection in everything she did. She never knew just what famous personality she would meet next. Last year she had met Ian Kingsley, the renowned photographer, when she had been sent to do an article on his home in Malibu. At 30 he had gained recognition as one of the leading photographers in America.

When she had first walked into his living room, which had a 180-degree view of the Pacific Ocean, she was completely overwhelmed with the brilliance of the way he had integrated the feeling of complete isolation from the everyday world with the warmth and naturalness of a livable, relaxing home. His mixing of a few treasured family antiques with modern furnishings had given the house a decidedly eclectic look. "Eclectic" was the one word he had objected to in the article, and Diana had willingly changed it. "The most overused and pretentious word today," he had said with a twinkle in his eye.

His home might have overwhelmed Diana, but Ian himself had completely taken her off guard. His muscular, rugged good looks—six-feet-four, dark curly hair, and mustache (plus the tan that went with living in the Pacific Ocean's backyard)—had made it difficult for Diana to concentrate on the interview, especially when he had concentrated so much on her face, telling her how exquisitely beautiful she was.

From that first meeting they had started dating, and for Ian it had been love at first sight. For the past eight years he had had an extremely difficult time relating to women in any long-term relationships. At 22 he had returned from Vietnam to find that his fiancee had married another man. The continued agony of having been jilted had become an emotion that had led him to feel he would never meet a woman he could completely trust. Then Diana had walked into his Malibu home, and he felt that here was a young woman who could bring back into his life a love he had thought would evade him forever.

Now, a year later, Diana believed that she too had fallen in love that day, but she was still unsure of marriage. She had experienced a great deal of heartache in her own life—her parents had been killed in a plane crash when she was 17. This had made her, of necessity, a very independent young woman. She had had to work her way through college and fend for herself, especially since her brother, James, an actor, had left for New York. Theirs had been an extremely happy childhood— the family was very close and Diana had wonderful memories of their years together. Their home had been a haven for her and James. Their parents, though strict, had shown them a love that even now she remembered as never restrictive, but one that had given assurance that they would always be there when needed. But now they were gone, and the enormous vacuum remained in her life.

Back in her office, Diana hastily tidied her desk. She would not be using it for more than a month, and the thought delighted her. It would be her first visit to England. She had heard so much about the country from her mother, who had been born there, that she felt as if she were going back to part of her roots. The only regret she had was that Ian was not going with her. Diana glanced at her watch. It was almost lunchtime and she was meeting him at the usual small bistro that had become a favorite rendezvous for them. She saw that she was running a few minutes late, so she quickly repaired her makeup. Then, brushing her hair without looking in a mirror, she rushed out of the office.

Ian was sitting at a table near the window, and Diana waved to him as she approached the bistro. He pointed to his watch and she gave a helpless sign with her hands, as if to say, "It's not my fault." Entering the restaurant, she went over and kissed him, murmuring, "Sorry, I had to finish an article."

He touched her hair and her cheek, saying, "That's okay, but I have to leave in half an hour. We're settling the book deal this afternoon at my agent's."

"Oh, how wonderful! I'm so excited for you!" Ian had been approached by a major publisher to do a collection of his magnificent photography.

Reaching out across the red-checked tablecloth, he took Diana's hand. "Do you know how much I'm going to miss you?" His face showed the extent to which he was dreading the separation. "I can't seem to concentrate on anything properly right now."

"I'll miss *you*, Ian." She squeezed his hand and once more tried to persuade him to change his schedule. "Why don't you fly over later and join me? We could have a wonderful time exploring London together.''

Obviously frustrated, he said regretfully, "You know I can't take time off right now—so much is happening.''

The waiter appeared and they ordered some cold consomme and a light salad. Ian instructed him that he had to leave very soon for an appointment, and could he please rush their order?

Ian buttered a roll with an intensity that showed how much he was feeling. "Diana, I'm serious now. Please give a lot of thought while you're away about our getting married.''

"I will, Ian. You know I love you—it's just that marriage is such a major step, and I'm not sure if I'm ready yet. I want it to be forever.''

"The feeling is mutual, Diana.'' Ian had seen too many marriages break up among the set he moved in. "I'll never get tired of waking up and seeing my beautiful wife next to me in bed.''

"I'm not that gorgeous first thing in the morning,'' Diana laughed, "so you'd better think twice about getting tied down to an early-morning disaster.''

"You, my darling, could never look like a disaster, no matter what time of day.'

The waiter returned with their lunch, and the conversation turned back to Ian's book and the photographs he felt should be included.

"I want them to put the one I took of you in

Carmel on the cover," he said determinedly.

Ian had photographed Diana silhouetted against the early-morning sky, leaning against the trunk of a gnarled cypress tree. The lighting and composition were superb. He had blown it up to poster size and had hung it in his living room. Diana's face had an almost ethereal expression and her hair had been caught by the capricious sea breeze, fanning it out into a radiant arc of light.

Ian kissed her hand and, though the bistro was crowded, they looked at each other in the way that those in love experience—oblivious of other people around them.

"I'm very flattered, Ian. Even if your publisher doesn't choose it, the fact that you would want that photograph on the cover means a great deal to me."

After Ian paid the bill, they walked out of the bistro into the sunlight of a hot Los Angeles afternoon. He put his arms around Diana and hugged her to him before they started walking back to her office hand in hand. They hardly talked— each one was thinking of the month-long separation.

When they reached Diana's office building, Ian said, "I'll be by your apartment to pick you up for the airport around 6 P.M. All right?" Diana nodded and kissed him tenderly.

"Thanks a lot...I love you." she whispered.

He watched her go through the revolving doors, then walked briskly to his appointment. His thoughts were only on Diana. Knowing her had changed his life completely. From a man who had distrusted the wiles of any woman for eight years after he had been jilted, he loved and had confidence in this beautiful, willowy, blonde young woman. She could be serious with him one moment, appreciating him and the quality of his work, then the next moment she would make him laugh with her impersonation of "El Crusto," her boss. They shared the humorous incidents that are only funny to those who enjoy a close relationship. Diana was tender, high-principled and at times fiery, but she was always able to lift Ian's spirits when he needed it.

Ian should have been feeling excited at the thought of a book being published. The agent had said that the publishing house would spare no expense in making the large-format volume a worthy showcase for his outstanding talent. But the thought of Diana leaving tonight made the book seem anticlimactic. Reaching his agent's office, he tried to put the thought of their parting at the back of his mind.

As Diana drove to her apartment in Brentwood, after finally saying her good-byes at the office, she realized that there was still so much to be done. Parking her white sports car, she ran up the steps to the apartment building talking to herself in the elevator.

"I must remember to pack my camera, my hair dryer..." She looked at her watch and saw that there was only half an hour to change and finish all the last-minute details.

Diana was about to put the key in the front door when it opened, and Sarah, with whom she shared the spacious apartment, was just on her way out. They had known each other in high school, and when the time came for Diana to find an apartment after her parents were killed, Sarah suggested that they move in somewhere together. She was an easy person to live with, as she seemed to be in another world most of the time. A little scatterbrained and living completely for her modeling career, this tall, striking brunette with enormous brown eyes seemed to be unaffected by temperament, and Diana appreciated their friendship.

"Oh, I'm so glad I got to see you before you left!" Sarah said in her low, breathy voice. "Have a wonderful time and do send me a postcard. If you meet any available dukes or earls, please send for me. I'd love to marry into the aristocracy!"

With a hug and a last-minute look in the mirror, Sarah rushed down the hallway and rang for the elevator. As she waited, she found time to do a few facial exercises while she ran in place. The awareness of her physical appearance was constant with her.

Diana laughed to herself as she shut the door and shook her head. She should probably exercise more herself, she thought, but tennis with Ian once or twice a week seemed to keep her figure in the shape he admired so often.

She changed quickly into a stunning casual outfit by Lauren. The red cotton bomber jacket, over a striped navy-and-white tee shirt and navy pants, together with red high-heeled sandals, made her look like a successful model. Her figure did justice to the clothes.

As she was packing the last few items, the doorbell rang. It was Ian, waiting to take her to the airport. She kissed him briefly, and as she turned to finish her packing he reached out for her and swept her back to him.

"These kisses are going to have to last me for a whole month, so none of your schoolgirl greetings..." His lips touched hers tenderly at first, then the feelings he had for Diana made the intensity of the kisses that followed more impassioned. Holding her close to him, he whispered, over and over again, "I love you, I love you, Diana."

The nearness of him made her forget the minutes ticking away and she murmured, "I love you too, Ian.'' She ran her hands though his crisp, curly hair—then rested her cheek against his. ''I'll be praying for both of us the whole time I'm away. This trip will be empty without you.'' She looked longingly into his eyes and they kissed again.

Ian released her, realizing that they would have to hurry or she would miss her plane.

His red Porsche wove in and out of the early-evening traffic. As Ian drove, Diana made sure her tickets and passport were in her handbag. When he pulled up at the TWA terminal, everything seemed to become so impersonal. There were so many details to take care of, but as the porter tagged her luggage for London Diana's heart started to beat faster.

''I really *am* like a schoolgirl, Ian. I still can't believe I'll really see Buckingham Palace and all that.''

Ian smiled wanly and leaned down to kiss her good-bye.

''Be sure to give the Queen my best regards.'' His attempt at humor betrayed how he was feeling. The sight of him looking so forlorn made Diana experience doubts about her trip; but then the porter's voice broke into her thoughts as he told her the gate number from which the plane to London would soon be leaving.

They had decided earlier that Ian would just

drop her off and not come to the plane, since the parking problems at the airport were so horrendous. Diana had said she preferred quick goodbyes anyway, so now they kissed briefly—but with intense feeling. She turned and waved to Ian as she waited for the glass entry doors to open. Then she was gone.

Ian drove off, feeling stunned and empty. He was glad that Diana had this opportunity to visit and work in England, but was conscious of an uneasy premonition that made him wonder if their lives would be quite the same when she returned.

That night, as he walked into his living room, he looked at the photograph of Diana hanging on the wall, and his loneliness overwhelmed him.

Chapter Two

~~~~~~~~

A light summer rain was falling in London when the taxi pulled up to Janet Nelson's early Victorian row house in Chelsea. The weather did not deter Diana's excitement for a moment. She had come armed with a raincoat, and her folding umbrella was packed in one of her suitcases.

Diana was prepared for the inevitable hazards of a British summer.

Janet Nelson had heard the taxi pull up and was already at the front door to welcome this young woman whom she had heard so much about over the years.

As Diana walked up the steps leading to her home, Janet was amazed at her beauty and her likeness to her mother. Pamela Lewis had been one of Janet's closest friends until she married an American and went to live in the United States.

"Welcome, dear Diana! I've been *so* looking forward to your visit. Sorry the weather didn't behave for you...it's been wretched all week."

Diana instantly felt at home with this attractive woman who had so graciously invited her to stay. In her late fifties and widowed, "Aunt" Janet looked like the perfect example of a well-to-do, well-dressed Englishwoman. Her dark hair, with flattering streaks of gray at the temples, was brushed back in a soft, becoming style. She was dressed in the understated tailoring of a top English designer.

Janet escorted Diana up to her room, which overlooked a small courtyard and was furnished in antiques and soft pastels. The two women talked at great length about Diana's mother. It was a welcome conversation, for so often Diana had longed to be able to speak to someone who had known her mother well.

In the small, elegant dining room they later continued their conversation over lunch.

"Your mother was always one for enjoying life to the fullest. You remind me so much of her, Diana." Her thoughts were miles away as she suddenly said, "Did she ever tell you about her trying to teach Sunday school and how our austere minister had to finally tell her that her exuberant personality was 'not in keeping with the qualifications required'?" She laughed as she remembered her friend's dismal failure when it came to keeping a class in order. "She entered the children's world, making everything such fun. Unfortunately, with her dismissal the children lost a very loving teacher."

Both Diana and Janet thought of their own loss when Pamela Lewis and her husband had been killed in the plane crash.

"There was a very beautiful memorial service for them in our church—Holy Trinity. I'd like to take you there if you have time one day."

"I'd like that, Aunt Janet."

Diana had always attended church with her parents, and at the time of their death the background of her faith had helped console her in her grief. Her busy schedule had somehow cut into any regular church attendance since then, and she often missed that weekly quiet time of being able to put everything into its right perspective.

The days began to pass quickly, and Diana felt more and more part of the London scene. Within walking distance from Sloane Square Station, Janet's house was in a perfect location. Diana was able to walk to her interview with the noted interior decorator who lived in Belgrave Square. Tom Bartlett, her editor, had warned her that he was known to be an extremely difficult man. But Diana seemed to be able to charm him, and the interview went well. She knew from the tapes she had made, plus her notes and some glorious photographs he had given her, that it would be a very good article.

Diana loved London and only wished that Ian could be with her. He was in her thoughts constantly, and she imagined how excited he would have been photographing the famous landmarks and the quaint and imposing facades of the houses.

Deep in thought, she made her way back to Janet Nelson's house. After walking for some time, she realized she had made a wrong turn and found herself on the busy Brompton Road. Diana took the opportunity to visit Harrod's department store, and, after admiring the quality and variety of merchandise it offered, she walked on in the direction of Chelsea. A sign across the street reading "Holy Trinity Church" reminded her that this was the church that Aunt Janet had mentioned. Diana crossed the bustling street and walked up the long path that led to the imposing edifice.

The great oak doors were open, and Diana walked hesitantly into the beautiful sanctuary. There was no one around except for the organist, who was quietly practicing. Diana recognized the melody as that of Bach's "Toccata and Fugue," and as the organist began to confidently play it, filling the church with the triumphant sound of the great composer's music, her heart ached. Sitting in a pew near the back of the church, her eyes on the altar with the light streaming through the magnificent stained-glass windows, she thought of her parents and the service that had been conducted here in their memory. Reaching for one of the hymnbooks, she turned to a hymn they had all loved to sing. Whispering it to herself, she read:

> The King of Love my Shepherd is,
> Whose goodness faileth never;
> I nothing lack if I am His,
> And He is mine forever.

The last line seemed to stand out to her as never before.

Diana's thoughts turned to Ian, and she asked God to help her decide whether she should marry Ian. He had never been against any of her beliefs, yet he had not had the same access that she had

had to Christianity. Deep down inside she always questioned whether she could be happily married to someone who did not completely share her faith.

Stepping out in the late-afternoon sunlight, Diana remained deep in thought. A longing to be with Ian enveloped her, and she seemed to miss him more each day. The hurrying crowds around her, some arm-in-arm—laughing together—accentuated her need for him. As she arrived back at Janet Nelson's house, she hoped there might be a letter from Ian, but there was none.

As soon as Janet heard the key in the door, she put her head around the living-room door and called, "There's been a change of plans, Diana." There was a note of excitement in her voice.

"Instead of dining out tonight, I'm having a few friends over."

Diana groaned inwardly. It had been a long day and she had hoped that, after a quiet, pleasant dinner at some small local Chelsea restaurant, she could have gone to bed early and recuperated from the long session she had had with the interior decorator.

Janet continued. "It all evolved over a telephone call I had this morning. My friend Lady Drayton was so interested when I was telling her about you that we decided it would be fun to have a spur-of-the-moment dinner party in your honor.''

Janet's voice was ecstatic as she named several people who were coming. "Some of them are around your own age, so it won't be just for old fogeys like me.''

The idea of Janet Nelson ever being an "old fogey" made Diana laugh. "You will never be that—you are too 'with it,' " she graciously told her hostess.

"Well, thank you, Diana. By the way, Lady Drayton's son Christopher will be coming. He is one of the most eligible bachelors in England, so you'd better watch out. He's terribly good-looking but has a reputation of being a playboy. He's broken many hearts.''

"I'll be on my guard.'' Diana laughed and thanked Janet for all the plans she had made. The long, luxurious bath that Diana had planned would have to be exchanged for a quick shower, she thought.

Promptly at 7:30 P.M. the guests started to arrive, and Diana was introduced to each one as "my dear late friend Pamela Lewis's daughter." Several had known Diana's mother and were "charmed to meet such a beautiful young woman." She had dressed in a white organza blouse which had exquisite embroidery across the bodice. The sleeves were full, caught at the wrist with a soft frill. The dramatic midlength black organza accentuated her lithe figure.

It was almost 8:30 P.M. when a knock at the front door heralded the arrival of Lord Christopher Drayton.

Smiling very self-assuredly, he said, "Frightfully sorry I am so late. The traffic in the King's Road was unbelievable."

Everyone else had come the same way and had not had any trouble, so there was a questioning look among the older guests that accented their disapproval. "Typical," murmured one of them within Christopher's hearing. He merely grinned and cheerfully ignored the criticism.

His parents, the Earl and Countess of Drayton, looked stoically at their son. For them he seemed an almost-lost cause—always late, forgetting important appointments, partying most nights, seemingly not intending to settle down. At 28 it was surely time for him to take on the responsibility that went with the family name.

The Earl and Countess of Drayton seemed to Diana as very down-to-earth people. Despite their wealth and titles, their attitude was one of warmth and caring. The earl in recent years had suffered with his health, which caused him to be even more concerned about the future of the Drayton family. Lady Drayton, a tall, stately woman who was caught up in the whirl of many charitable organizations, was obviously drawn to Diana and watched, seemingly offhandedly, as her son talked animatedly to her.

As soon as he had entered the room, Christopher had spotted Diana, and with a few perfunctory "hellos" to the other guests, he demanded to be introduced to this "gorgeous visitor from the States."

In spite of Janet's warnings, Diana found herself immediately attracted to this handsome, fair-haired young man. He had tremendous charm. Elegantly dressed, in a Savile Row-tailored, dark gray suit, he was the epitome of sophistication—yet there was an air of boyish enthusiasm about him. As he talked to Diana, he made her feel as if she were the only person in the room. Seated next to her through dinner, he monopolized and delighted her with his witty conversation.

"Why don't you come and visit us for a few days at the castle? My mother would love to have you stay, wouldn't you, Mama?" Lady Drayton agreed and thought it "a splendid idea." Seeing Diana's hesitation, Christopher pressed the invitation. "I absolutely insist."

"Would you mind very much, Aunt Janet?"

"Of course not. It would be a wonderful experience for you. Their castle was originally built in the 1400s, so you wouldn't have anything like it in the States." Of course Janet realized that there might be other reasons why Diana would enjoy a visit to the castle, but she kept those thoughts to herself.

"I still have an assignment that I have to take care of—the *real* reason for my being in this country." Diana explained to Christopher that she was to interview Jason Winter, the playwright.

"I know him well," said Christopher. "As a matter of fact, he lives only a few miles from us. I could take you over any day—so you see there's positively no excuse. Why don't I pick you up tomorrow afternoon around three and we can plan to arrive at Drayton in time for dinner?"

Swept along by his enthusiasm, Diana agreed. Her vacation had taken on a very different course, but it would be intriguing to see how the aristocracy lived firsthand—and with such an amusing and attractive host.

★   ★   ★

It was almost dusk when Christopher's car turned into the impressive driveway framed by enormous wrought-iron gates leading to Castle Drayton. Diana saw the castle rising high up on a hill, looking as it must have done for centuries— proudly dominating the countryside, its massive walls giving a feeling of permanence. Lights were sparkling from its windows, and as they drove

along the drawbridge, suspended across the moat
which surrounded the castle, Diana felt as if she
were entering another world.

Lady Drayton greeted them enthusiastically.
"How lovely that you could be with us, Diana!
Christopher, do take her up to her room—I'm
sure you would like to freshen up before dinner.
We'll be dining in about half an hour."

As she entered her bedroom, Diana noticed the
twilight casting beautiful patterns over the carpet
as its misty shafts shone through the diamond-
paned windows. The four-poster bed, with its
voluminous rose-pink silk canopy, looked as it
must have done centuries before. Diana instantly
loved the room. Its furnishings, though most of
them antique, seemed to welcome her, and she
knew she would enjoy her stay in such a magnificent setting.

★　　★　　★

The days sped by, and Diana found Christopher's company more and more pleasurable.
Thoughts of Ian were with her, but she had re-
solved that just for these few weeks—which she
knew could only be a wonderful interlude in her
life—she would accept the friendship that Christopher offered.

A telephone call by him to Jason Winter set up
a luncheon appointment and a time for Diana to

interview him. His Georgian house proved to be just as glorious as the photographs she had seen. The restoration had been as perfect as was possible, leaving much of the original intact.

Walking through the spectacular gardens, which were laid out in an early-eighteenth-century manner, Diana asked Jason Winter many pertinent questions—all the time very conscious of the fact that she was being watched by Christopher from the terrace. She was becoming increasingly aware of his interest in her—the way he looked at her, with his eyes following her every move, and the touch of his hand on hers sending a sensation of excitement coursing through her body.

Chapter Three

In the reflection of the eighteenth-century gilded mirror, Diana finished brushing her long blonde hair. There was a wistfulness about her expression, for this would be the last night spent at Castle Drayton—after two glorious weeks. Her visit to England had been a wonderful one, one

31

which had found her irresistibly drawn to the heir to this incredible castle. Now tomorrow would find her flying back over the Atlantic, to her apartment in Los Angeles.

"Such different worlds," thought Diana as she surveyed the oak-paneled guest room. "I want to remember everything about this place forever."

As she sat before the antique mirror, her imagination pictured other young women, centuries before, dressing for a ball in the beautiful gowns of long ago.

A soft tap at the door brought her back to reality, and she rose quickly to answer it. Christopher's finely chiseled features and captivating smile were silhouetted in the light coming from the hallway. Dressed in evening attire, he looked extraordinarily handsome. His brown eyes flashed in appreciation.

"Diana, you look even more beautiful tonight. I don't think I'm going to allow you to leave tomorrow."

Diana was wearing a dress that she had bought at Harrod's only the afternoon before. Christopher had driven her up to London, and after tea in the formal restaurant of the renowned department store he had left her to shop while he attended to some family business. She had seen the dress and been completely captivated by the exquisite, gossamerlike material. Spun with threads of silver, the pale blue floral pattern matched her intensely lovely eyes.

Standing at the bedroom door, with Christopher's hand in hers, Diana looked like a portrait from the past. Her soft shoulders rose above the deep frill, which was gathered by a blue satin ribbon echoing the wide sash. As they walked down the high arched hallway and passed the family portraits, the skirt billowed and the silver threads shimmered in the candlelight.

"Tonight," thought Diana, "I feel as if I belong here!"

She felt Christopher's admiring glances and the tightening of his hand in hers.

"After dinner I want to have a long talk with you, Diana."

Their eyes met and a feeling of deep longing swept over her. As they descended the wide baroque staircase, voices could be heard coming from the family living room. The Earl and Countess of Drayton were entertaining their guests. Diana managed to regain her composure as she and Christopher entered the room.

All eyes turned toward her as Lady Drayton exclaimed, "How lovely you look, Diana! Come, meet our guests." Turning to Christopher, she said, "You introduce her to them...they've all been looking forward to meeting your delightful guest from the States."

Christopher showed great pride as he introduced Diana to these people, many of whom he
had know all his life. He had warned Diana that
some of them were "crashing bores" and to take
no notice if they appeared to be rather "anti-
American."

"Some of them are still fighting the revolution
in their own way," he had laughingly remarked.

As Diana encountered each one, she felt as if
she were being analyzed and graded, and was
greatly relieved when the butler announced to
Lady Drayton that "Dinner is served, m'lady."
Christopher offered Diana his arm, and together
they followed the guests into the vast dining hall
of Castle Drayton. The family banners were
draped on either side of the enormous stone
fireplace, where, even though it was summer, an
enormous fire blazed—taking the chill from the
cavernous, vaulted room.

To Diana's right was seated a rather large, pom-
pous brigadier, who seemed to attack his food as
though he were still on the battlefield. Small talk
was exceedingly difficult, until Diana happened
to mention a battle that the brigadier had been
involved in—the Battle of the Bulge.

"Ah, yes, I have good memories of those days,
and your countrymen. Ah, yes, yes indeed," and
he continued to devour his roast beef. Christopher, seated to her left, kept making pointed

remarks under his breath about the appropriateness of the name of the battle as connected with the vast gentleman, and Diana found it extremely difficult to keep a straight face throughout the long and enormous meal.

Finally, after dessert, Christopher asked Lady Drayton if they could be excused as this was Diana's last night in England. Graciously she agreed, and they escaped the after-dinner talk that would go on indefinitely.

As soon as the huge dining room door had closed, Christopher took Diana off guard as he kissed her. Then, taking her by the hand, he ran with her down the long hallway, both of them stifling laughter until they turned the corner.

"You were unforgivable at dinner, Chris. I didn't know where to look most of the time!"

"I told you some of them would be rather boring, but I never dreamed Mama would seat you next to the brigadier!" Changing his tone completely, he said to her seriously, "Diana, let's go to the library and talk. There's so much I want to say and so little time left."

With his arms around her shoulders, they walked past the statues that seemed to stand guard in the half-light, and entered the library. It was a long, lofty room with bookshelves from floor to ceiling. Rare and beautifully bound leather books lined the shelves. In the center of the west wall was a large marble fireplace; two chintz-covered sofas in front of it faced each other. Between them was a long, low table with magazines and a beautiful arrangement of roses.

Diana sank down into the cushions of one of the sofas, but Christopher remained standing with his back to the fireplace. There was a long pause as he stared at Diana, not quite knowing how to begin the conversation.

Gazing into the fire, Diana thought again of how her vacation in England had taken such a completely different course since she had met Christopher. Now tomorrow she would leave the castle and be met in Los Angeles by Ian. Deep down inside she felt guilty at the way she had allowed herself to become so attracted to Christopher. He came and sat down beside her. Taking her hands, he looked into her eyes and said, "Diana, remember when I told you I was going to take care of some family business yesterday while we were at Harrod's?" She nodded. "Well, it wasn't quite true. I went down to the jewelry department and found something for you."

Reaching into his breast pocket, he pulled out a deep-blue velvet box. "I wanted you to have something to remember your stay here."

Surprised, Diana said, "Chris, how kind of you!"

Her hands seemed to tremble as she took his

gift. Opening it, she saw a beautiful gold-chain bracelet lying in the satin folds of the box. Diana was speechless. Christopher leaned over and picked up the bracelet.

"Let me read the inscription to you." He turned over the exquisite locket, and there on the back was engraved, "To Diana—Forever, Chris."

She was taken completely by surprise. "Thank you, Chris...but I really don't think I can accept it. You know about Ian..."

"Yes, I do, but I wanted you to know how *I* feel." Seeing her hesitation, he said, "At least accept it as a remembrance of your visit here."

Diana felt embarrassed, yet she did not want to offend him. "Well, each time I look at it I will remember the wonderful time I've had. Thank you, Chris."

"Diana"—his voice was very tense—"please don't talk as if we are never going to see each other again. I want to see you and be with you al—" He stopped before he could say the word "always." Ever since he was a child it had been drummed into him that he would have to marry someone in his own set. Bloodlines were extremely important, but seated next to this vibrant, beautiful young woman he found it difficult to control his strong emotions. He took Diana in his arms.

"You might as well know, Diana, I've fallen in love with you. I want you to be my wife."

She broke away from him. "Chris, isn't this all too sudden?"

"Why should it be? I knew the night we met at Janet's that you were that very special person I had been looking for."

In spite of the intensity of his speech and the very romantic setting, Diana threw back her head and laughed.

"Aren't you taking a great deal for granted, Lord Christopher Drayton? I haven't said yes yet!"

He stood and brought Diana up to him. His arms held her tightly and she felt as if she could not breathe, her heart was pounding so.

"Please say yes," he whispered as he kissed her tenderly. "I do want you to be my wife. One day we will be the master and mistress of this castle. Diana, it would be so empty if you were not with me."

His hands moved across her shoulders, touching her long blonde hair. "I can't think of seeing you off on that plane tomorrow, without knowing that you will come back to me."

Diana turned from him trying to rationalize all that had happened in such a short time. "Chris, I must have time to think. There is so much that needs sorting out in my life. I believed I really did love Ian, and he is expecting an answer when I go back tomorrow." She could tell that Chris was not listening to her as he came over and kissed her again. Breaking away, she said, "Let me run upstairs and change and we'll go for a walk. I need to have some fresh air and time to think."

"Good idea...but first wouldn't you like me to put your bracelet on for you?"

"Oh, yes. Thank you again, Chris. I shall really treasure it." But she still felt uneasy about accepting it as he put it on her wrist.

When Diana arrived downstairs a few minutes later dressed in jeans and a light sweater, Chris was already waiting for her. He had changed into some old gray flannels and a plaid shirt that had seen better days.

"That shirt looks as if it should have been thrown out years ago," Diana laughingly remarked.

"It should have been, but it's one of my favorites. Mama is always having a fit when I wear it. Makes the family look rather impoverished... but *I like it*!" he said humorously.

He opened a door leading to the terrace, and as they passed the living room windows, where the guests were now seated, they tiptoed quietly so as not to be seen.

"Let's go down by the lake, Chris. It's so beautiful. I wish I had photographed it."

"I shall see to it that photos will be sent to you in Los Angeles. In fact, I shall keep sending you photos of the whole place, so that you will feel dreadfully homesick and want to take the first plane back here.''

Diana laughed. She delighted in his carefree and forthright manner. She would have expected someone from the English aristocracy to always be starchy, but Chris was anything but that.

Hand in hand Diana and Chris walked silently on the lawn which led down to the lake. The moon was reflected in the shimmering waters, and as if by command three white swans swam toward them, expecting to be fed.

Diana sat down by the water's edge and Chris joined her. She kept looking at the bracelet. ''It's so beautiful...I still can't get over it.''

''I hope you never do.''

''I don't think I ever will.'' Her heart began to pound as he put his arms around her, and with her head on his shoulder they studied the peaceful scene. The tall trees that surrounded the lake were now like dark sentinels against the backdrop of the moonlit sky.

''I would like to stay here all night,'' Diana thought.

As if he knew what she was thinking, Chris said, ''If we stay here too long we'll get rather damp, I'm afraid. The English dew is known for its penetrating powers.''

''Penetrating powers or not, I love it here, so

please let's stay for a while. We still have so much to talk about. You really did all the talking in the library, so now it's my turn."

"All right, fire away. I shall object most strongly, though, if you turn me down, and my feelings will be radically hurt." He said this with a smile, but Diana detected a look of sadness in his eyes.

"Chris, I'm not turning you down. It's just that it's all so sudden—I need some time to think. This stay with you has been an almost enchanted time for me. Now I have to go back to the reality of my life in California. Perhaps then we can both see things as they really are."

"You mean I should go back with you? I'll pack immediately!"

"No!" For all the seriousness of the situation, Diana could not help laughing once more. This is what she really liked about him—he made her laugh. Ian was usually so intense, and laughter did not come easily to him. But could laughter be enough on which to build a marriage? Would the fact that she was so incredibly attracted to Chris be sufficient foundation for a life together? Ian loved her, and she knew that this love was deep and sincere. Was Chris just enamored by her, or did he really love her too?

Diana turned from the lake and looked at the great castle. Its turrets gleamed in the moonlight and the windows shone like jewels. It seemed like a painting from the fifteenth century. Diana's eyes rested on the chapel. She had visited there several times on her own. Sitting in the old pews, her thoughts had turned to her childhood. She remembered that when she was 14 her mother had taken her for a drive up the California coastline and they had parked overlooking the Pacific Ocean. It was a magnificent scene as the surf pounded the cliffs below, and it was indelibly imprinted on her mind. Her mother had talked to her about the future, about her one day finding the young man she would marry.

Realizing that several moments had gone by in silence, Diana said, "Chris, my mother prayed with me a few years before she was killed for the person whom God had chosen for me. Mother said, 'Diana, just imagine, out there in this world is a young man growing up who will one day be your husband. Let's pray for him and for you—that together you will find happiness.' " Diana paused for a few seconds. "Tonight I remember that scene so vividly and I wonder...are you or Ian the person who we were praying for? Are you the one who God intends for me to marry?"

Her eyes were wet with tears, for the memory of her mother and her deep faith made Diana long to be able to talk with her.

Chris's voice brought her thoughts back to him.

"Diana, how beautiful your mother must have been! I'm glad you shared that time you spent together with me."

He paused, finding it difficult to find the right words. "I don't really have the kind of faith you do. Perhaps I envy you in a way. When I was very young, I remember I did." Looking over at the castle, he reflected, "But later I thought our chapel was something left over from the medieval times. It has always been there and so I suppose I have taken it for granted. It's been used for weddings and christenings and occasions like that, but it hasn't been very important in my life, much to my mother's chagrin."

He threw a stone into the lake and watched the ripples grow larger and larger, his thoughts drifting away with them.

"At boarding school I had to attend services every morning and I can tell you when religion is rammed down your throat—especially when it's so cold you can hardly bear to sit and listen to a ponderous old parson going on about sin and the wickedness of your ways—well, all I wanted to do was to get out of there as fast as I could run. I felt stifled."

Diana's thoughts were racing. She wondered why she had shared such a personal memory with him. Sensing her embarrassment, Chris said tenderly, "Forgive me, Diana, I don't want you to think I don't respect what your mother prayed for...I only hope *I* was the subject of that prayer."

Diana turned to him and instinctively put her arms around him, burying her face against his chest.

For several minutes they stood there, not wanting to draw apart. Diana felt the warmth of his body against her and it seemed as if nothing else really mattered but the two of them. Was it guilt or was it love for Ian that brought thoughts of him to her...even as Chris kissed her?

Chapter Four

~~~~~~~~~~~~~~~~

The sound of guests leaving the castle (as their cars were driven down the long driveway that led through the woods to the nearby village of Drayton) made Diana realize that the hour was late and that she still had to finish packing.

"Chris, I really should go back and get ready for the flight tomorrow."

Reluctantly he started to walk with her, his mind still on what she had confided to him. She had not committed herself to him but neither had she refused him. At least he had something to be grateful for, but he felt troubled. Ian was obviously a very strong rival. Chris looked at Diana as they walked across the lawn and thought about the faith that had been important to her family life and still remained strong in spite of the fact that her parents had been killed so tragically.

He stopped walking and said suddenly, "Diana, where does your belief about God and His concern for you stand when you have lost two people who were so important in your life? I mean, do you really feel that God cares for you even though they have been taken away?"

Diana looked at him thoughtfully and took his hands in hers. "Chris, I don't have all the answers. I only know that my mother and father believed that death is not the end—it is only a beginning. I still long to see them and...," looking away, she continued softly, "...I often feel very empty inside, but I have not grieved for them without the hope of knowing I will see them again one day."

"Then you really think there is an afterlife?"

"Yes, very definitely."

Chris was about to say something when some of the guests saw them and waved. Their serious moments ended when the Earl and Countess of Drayton beckoned them over and they went to join them.

"Diana, my dear," called the earl, "we are going to miss your lovely face around here. I wish you could have stayed with us longer."

"So do I , Lord Drayton. I have loved every minute of these last two weeks. I would like to thank you and Lady Drayton for your kindness to me."

Lady Drayton smiled and said, "Diana, you are welcome *any* time to come and stay. I know Christopher would agree with me, wouldn't you?" She turned to him with a twinkle in her eye.

Chris smiled at his parents, and with his arm around Diana's shoulders he said, "It certainly wouldn't be a hardship to have Diana around..." He wanted to say "always."

Lady Drayton looked at Chris's tattered shirt and said, "I'm sure Diana would have a very good influence on your wardrobe, which would be most welcome."

Diana straightened his threadbare collar and they laughed.

The butler came to the terrace and said to Diana, "Miss, there is a telephone call for you. Would you please take it in the living room?"

"Thank you, Edwards." Diana stopped to look at Chris for a second, then excused herself to his parents as she walked into the living room and picked up the telephone.

"Hello?"

"Diana, it's Aunt Janet. I wanted to talk to you before you left, but first—there is a cable for you. Should I open it?"

"Oh, please do, Aunt Janet, and I'm sorry I've not called you. Chris has kept me so busy that I didn't realize the time had gone by so quickly."

"I can imagine," laughed Janet. She opened the cable and read, "Missing you so STOP Will meet your plane STOP Magazine has us both on assignment in San Francisco STOP Delighted STOP All my love Ian."

There was a long pause before Diana said anything. The cable had brought her back to the world of California, and she was not sure whether she welcomed it. "Thank you," she said faintly.

"Are you feeling all right?" asked Janet.

"Oh, fine, thanks. I guess it made me realize even more that my vacation is well and truly over. Aunt Janet, thank you again for inviting me— even though I didn't stay with you as long as we expected!"

After a few more minutes' conversation, Diana hung up deep in thought. Chris came in and saw her standing there, unaware of his presence.

"Diana...I hope it wasn't bad news."

"Oh, no. Just Aunt Janet calling to say good-
bye."

Already Ian was coming between them, for
Diana was now very conscious that the next few
days would be spent in close proximity with him
as they worked together in San Francisco. She did
not want to mention the cable to Chris, as it would
only spoil the last few hours they had together.

Chris sensing that something was wrong, said,
"How about some hot chocolate and a quick chat
by the fire before you go upstairs?"

"That sounds wonderful. I still feel a bit
chilled from that English dew. I should have
listened to your warning."

Chris rang for the butler and asked that hot
chocolate be served in the library for the two of
them, and then escorted Diana there. He went
over to the stereo and put on Rachmaninoff's
Symphony No. 2. They had played it together
many times. Now, sitting by the hearth of the
great fireplace, they were silent as the theme from
the Adagio seemed to sweep over them and
permeate the room with its tragically beautiful
melody.

A knock at the door interrupted their thoughts
and a doorman entered with a silver tray on
which was a large pot of hot chocolate, together with a dish of petits fours. He set

the tray down on the low table near the fire.

"Will that be all, sir?"

"Yes, thank you, Davis. That's fine."

After the doorman left, Chris leaned over and poured a cup for Diana and himself. Looking at her pensively, he said, "I will not enjoy my nightly ritual of hot chocolate again until you are back here with me."

Diana just looked at him and said a quiet "Thank you" as he handed her a cup. The music continued to accompany their mood as they drank the welcome beverage. Chris looked at Diana and noticed the way the firelight made her blonde hair shine like a golden halo.

"Rachmaninoff must have known what it was like to say good-bye to someone he loved." His fingers traced over her eyebrows and down her intangibly provocative nose, and then lingered for a moment on her lips. "Oh, how I wish you didn't have to go back tomorrow! Can't you cable your magazine and tell them you're staying longer?"

"No, Chris. I really can't, much as I would love to, but they're depending on me to go on an assignment as soon as I get back."

She put her cup down on the tray. As she rose she said, "I really must go to bed now. I'll never be able to get up in the morning, and we'll have to leave very early for the airport."

"Very well. May I see you to your room?"

Chris jumped up and kissed her gently on the cheek.

As they went up the great staircase, the old grandfather clock struck one, and its methodical ticking seemed to make the time they still had together even more fleeting.

When they arrived at Diana's bedroom door Chris said, "Could we have an early breakfast together? Say about 6:30? I want to spend all the time I can with you."

"Yes, Chris, of course. That sounds wonderful, even though you know how much I hate breakfast!" She smiled and put her arms around his neck. "It isn't going to be easy to say goodbye to you. Meeting you and spending this time here has been one of the most wonderful things that has happened to me."

Chris started to say something, but she put her fingers over his lips. "We've just got to wait and see how we feel about each other when we're apart. I have to be sure I would love you for yourself, not for other reasons—this castle, your family, everything else. I have to be able to look at it all objectively. What I'm trying to say is to be patient with me, give me a little time."

Chris leaned down to Diana and looked into her eyes as he said, "I'll give you time, but not very long. I've never felt so sure about anything in my whole life—I love you, Diana."

They kissed deeply and longingly, and finally Diana pulled herself away.

"See you in the morning...in just a very few hours."

Diana shut the door and leaned against it. Her heart was racing again and she had the overwhelming desire to open the door and call him back. She already missed the exciting yet tender feelings that his presence stirred in her.

Still thinking of him she crossed to the window and sat for a minute looking out over the lake. The moon was obliterated by a cloud for a moment, then it appeared and illuminated the water—bringing back memories of their time together as she had confided to Chris. He had not laughed at her even though he did not share her beliefs.

She went over to the dressing table and took off her watch. It was already 1:30 A.M. Looking over at her suitcases, she realized that the maid had done most of the packing for her. The navy blue suit with the white ruffled georgette blouse still hung in the armoire. Her red high-heeled shoes and handbag were also there. She had decided earlier to wear this outfit on the plane.

"Wonderful," thought Diana as she undressed, "wonderful to have a maid. I'd never have to pack again." This independent young woman was gradually getting used to the idea of being waited on.

She set her travel alarm clock for 5:30 A.M.

and groaned, realizing how short the night would be. As she climbed into the vast canopied bed her thoughts turned to Ian's telegram. In just a few hours she would be seeing him, but so much had happened to her that she wondered just how she would be able to tell him about it all. They had been so close, and above all she did not want to hurt this man, who really seemed to love her. She brushed her hair away from her eyes, and as she did so the gold bracelet touched her cheek, reminding her of Chris. Turning over the locket, she read the inscription again: "To Diana— Forever, Chris." "Forever" kept coming back to her. As she fell asleep she prayed that somehow she would be very sure about the decision she would have to be making.

When the alarm clock went off, she awoke with a start, remembering that now, so soon, she would be leaving the castle—and Chris.

Diana showered and dressed quickly and ran down the stairs, looking for him. The small family dining room, where breakfast was usually served, was deserted and there was no sign of anyone. Then she heard voices out on the terrace, and there was Chris supervising the breakfast, which had been set for two on a small round table. At the center of the crisp white tablecloth were fresh flowers in a crystal vase, picked by Chris moments before. A single red rose was on the napkin on her plate. Diana kissed and thanked him for the thought. "My breakfasts in Los Angeles are never as romantic as this."

"I hope they never will be, unless I'm with you."

Chris seated her, and as he passed by to sit opposite her, he kissed the back of her neck. Diana picked up the rose and smelled it, then whispered, "It's lovely."

"I didn't order any eggs or bacon or the whole traditional English breakfast. I thought you wouldn't be able to face all that at such an early hour." Taking off the lid of a silver dish, he continued, "I thought you would like these strawberries—handpicked by yours truly."

"How wonderful! You must have been up for ages to have done all this!"

"I know how much you love them, Diana."

Over coffee, strawberries and cream, and toast with marmalade they talked quietly, looking out on the beautifully landscaped grounds of the castle. The morning mist still lingered in the trees as the summer sun began its hazy ascent, promising that the day would be one of those rare glorious English events.

"What will you do now, Chris—I mean, after I've gone?"

"Well, my father is teaching me more and more

about how to manage the estate, so my days will be mostly taken up with that. He is thinking of opening part of the castle to the public. The taxes and upkeep are making it increasingly difficult for us. Mother hates the idea of enormous coaches arriving with hordes of tourists but it would be a way of being able to keep the ancestral home." Passing her another piece of toast, he said, "Just think—when you come back we may put you to work as a tour guide!"

Diana laughed. "What do you think about it all?"

"It really doesn't worry me. I love meeting people, and after all I feel part of it is theirs— it's part of English history."

"That's a very democratic way of looking at it." Diana thought for a moment, then continued, "The castle is really so beautiful that it would be great to be able to share it with so many people."

"Well, of course we'd only open the east wing, which would still give us our privacy. Anyway, we usually move back to our house in London at the end of September and get ready for the season—what's left of it, that is. Part of me loves the city life, probably because most of my friends are there."

His voice trailed off, and both of them knew that they were thinking of the last few hours they had left together.

Chris changed his light tone of voice to one or urgency. "Diana, you will never know how much I wanted to come back to your room last night."

Diana, remembering how she had felt when she closed the door, thought, "And you will never know how much I wanted you to..."

Chris came around to her chair and tilted her face up to his. "What would have happened if I had done so?"

"Chris, if we do make love I want to be your wife."

"Another part of your belief?"

"Yes, and don't think it's easy—it isn't. I have all the deep longings and desires that most people have. It's just..."

"Just what?"

"Something very special and wonderful to me. Do you understand?"

"Strangely enough, I do, difficult as it is."

Their conversation was interrupted by Edwards, who came to the terrace. "Lord Christopher, excuse me, but you and Miss Lewis should be leaving for the airport in about 15 minutes."

"Oh, very good, thank you, Edwards. The time seems to be racing ahead of us."

Diana got up from her chair and whispered, "Thank you for understanding." Picking up the rose, she left for her room. Quickly she put the flower between the pages of a magazine and packed it in her suitcase. Once more she walked over to the window; her thoughts raced as she felt all the deep emotion of leaving this wonderful place and Chris. Turning, she picked up her handbag and jacket and walked quickly out of the room and down the long corridor, where only last night she had walked with Chris and their feelings for each other had been translated in their nearness.

The footman passed her on his way to her room to get the luggage, and she smiled at him. "Thank you, Davis, for everything."

"It's been a real pleasure to have you here, miss. We all hope you'll be back soon."

"I hope so too."

Diana ran down the stairs, and there was Chris and the Earl and Countess of Drayton waiting by the open door.

"Remember, Diana, we all loved having you here. Take the first opportunity you can to return." Lady Drayton had been exceptionally warm to Diana, something that Chris was very quick to notice. Perhaps she sensed in Diana a depth that so few of Christopher's other girlfriends seemed to have. Maybe being from an old established English family was not as important after all... Lady Drayton kissed Diana on the cheek and the Earl did the same. "Hurry back, my dear," he said emphatically.

"Thank you again for everything."

Chris opened the door of his dark green Jaguar, and she slipped into the soft leather bucket seat reluctantly. He closed the door and got in on the driver's side. As he turned the key to start the engine, he gave Diana a long, thoughtful look.

"To the airport, madam?"

Diana nodded sadly and turned to wave to his parents. She felt as if she were leaving her family. "How strange," she thought; "I've only known them two weeks."

The car sped down the long driveway, shaded intermittently from the morning sun by the tall, aged oak trees. As they approached the magnificent wrought-iron gates, Diana said, "Chris, would you stop for a moment?"

"Of course. What is it? Did you forget something?"

"No, I just wanted to look at the castle once more."

Turning in her seat, she looked through the back window of the car and saw the castle rising high on the hill. It gave Diana a feeling that no matter what might happen, it would be waiting for her. She turned back to Chris and kissed him on the cheek. "All right, I'm ready to face the world again."

"You really love that old castle, don't you?"

Diana nodded. The sense of history within its

walls and the warmth of the Drayton family had had a tremendous effect on her, one that would go with her to California. Most of all, the feeling of almost belonging to a family once more seemed to fill the agonizing void she had experienced.

They drove through the picturesque village of Drayton, with its thatched roof cottages and the quaint little tea shop that they had stopped at last week. Its low, mullioned windows, in which tempting cakes and scones were displayed, had made Chris and Diana decide to have tea there. In the low-beamed ceiling shop, with the blue-and-white gingham tablecloths, they had laughed over tea and her "So *these* are crumpets!" Diana had admired the blue-and-white china, and Chris on the way out had bought her a cup and saucer to remember their visit. The gift was now safely packed in one of her suitcases.

The Jaguar passed the village green, where they had stopped to watch a game of cricket and Chris had explained to her the intricacies of the sport. Diana had delighted in watching the locals sitting in deck chairs with newspapers over their faces, sleeping in the summer sun. When an "Oh, well played, sir" was shouted sufficiently loud enough to awaken them, they would sit up suddenly, discarding their newspapers—and applaud also, muttering their appreciation of such fine sportsmanship. The villagers all knew Chris, and he had introduced Diana to some of them, who had looked at her most admiringly.

Now Chris and Diana entered the major highway that would take them to Heathrow Airport. Neither had spoken for a while. As they held hands, Diana looked at Chris as he concentrated on the road ahead. She noticed how his hair curled over the top of his collar. His mother had insisted that he go to the barber before the dinner at the castle, but he had conveniently forgotten.

"Don't forget to have your hair trimmed, will you?" Diana touched the back of his neck. Chris laughed and said, "I may wait until you get back."

Before the car came to the highway he stopped at the side of the road. Turning to Diana, he pulled her close to him. "We've got a few minutes and I know the airport is going to be absolute bedlam." He looked at her intensely, trying to take in every detail of her face. He wanted to remember the way her eyes lit up when she looked at him (the blue reminding him of the color in the tapestries at the castle) and the way the tip of her nose moved when she smiled.

"Diana, darling Diana, I'm going to miss you so terribly." They kissed, and their longing for each other seemed to transcend time.

A few minutes later Chris started the engine, and as they drove onto the highway they were immediately surrounded by a stream of cars and trucks. As they went through the tunnel leading to the airport, Diana shouted, "You will write, won't you?"

"Of course!" Chris shouted back. "And I'll phone as often as I can."

Now they were completely caught up in the parking and airport procedure. The Jaguar pulled up to the overseas building and a smiling porter came up to the car.

"Need some 'elp, sir?"

Chris nodded and got out to unlock the trunk of the car. Diana's suitcases were put on a trolley, and with a promise of "See you inside, sir," the porter walked quickly into the building.

Chris said, "I'll go and park while you get checked in. I'll be as quick as possible."

Diana walked to the door of the building and followed the path of the porter. He was standing in line for her at one of the airline counters.

"Looks like you've got caught up in a tour group, miss. Would you like me to stay and 'elp you?"

Diana assured him that she would be able to manage and gave him a generous tip. "Thank you very much, miss. I 'ope you and your 'usband have a good flight.''

His words made her feel even more desolate, but she didn't bother to explain that they weren't married. At that moment she rather liked his mistaken assumption.

At last she was checked in, and Chris came flying through the doors looking for her. She had already felt lost without him for those few minutes. He put his arm around her shoulders and they walked slowly to the security area. "No Visitors Beyond This Point." They clung to each other, not caring what anyone thought.

In a choked voice Diana said, "Thank you again, Chris, for everything and for this." She touched the bracelet.

"I'm counting on you making a very fast decision, darling. God love you and keep you safe."

"You too, Chris."

Their final kiss made an elderly American couple turn around as they were going through security. "My, my," said the man admiringly, but his wife was not so sure.

Diana walked to the barrier, and waved goodbye, and then was gone down the long corridor. She felt as if she were leaving someone she had known and loved all her life. Tears were in her eyes as she continued walking to the plane.

Chris turned and walked out of the building, feeling incredibly lost. Getting into his car, he drove off in a daze. The beautiful girl who had been by his side in the car only a few minutes before was now preparing to board a plane that would take her 6000 miles away from him. He turned on the radio and found some loud, blaring music—anything to keep him from feeling so empty. Looking up, he noticed a piece of paper tucked in the sun visor. He reached for it and recognized Diana's handwriting. She had written him a quick note while he was distracted by the porter. Even though the traffic was bearing down on him on all sides, he opened the note. With one hand on the wheel and one eye on the road, he read:

> Chris darling,
>   Thank you for the most wonderful two weeks of my life. You are so dear. God bless...
>
> Love, Diana
>
> P.S. How about visiting your friendly neighbourhood chapel sometime?

In spite of his loneliness, Chris laughed. He would never take the chapel for granted again... Diana had begun to make him realize the meaning of its presence.

Chapter Five

Diana fastened her seat belt and looked out the window of the plane. She was fortunate in getting a window seat, and it seemed that the seat next to her was going to be vacant. She didn't feel like talking to anyone, which was unusual for her, but today the thought of leaving Chris made her

want to just quietly contemplate all that had
happened in such a short time.

As she watched the luggage being loaded onto
the giant jet, she thought that to everyone else it
was just another normal day. The stewardesses
were busy seeing that everything was in order
before takeoff. Diana felt like saying, "Wait a
minute! I've changed my mind—I want to get off!
I want to hurry back to Chris and feel his arms
around me again." But she knew that this was
impossible. She had to face Ian and all that lay
ahead in America.

"Would you all please take your seats and
prepare for takeoff..." The stewardess's voice
made Diana realize that she was now saying
farewell to England. The huge jet's engines roared
and the plane made its way down the runway. As
it ascended, she watched the English streets
become small winding ribbons and the cars and
buses turn into toys that had been wound up by
a child's hand. Now the meadows, fringed by
hedgerows, took on the pattern of a patchwork
quilt. The steeple of a country church came into
view, and she felt she could have leaned out of
the window and picked it up with her hands. The
sight of it calmed her, for ever since her parents
had been killed, flying had been a difficult experience for her. She had tried to overcome her
fears as her job took her to so many cities in the

States, but she still felt a certain fear each time she took off or landed in a plane.

Diana wondered where Chris was as he drove back to the castle. Had he seen her hastily scribbled note? "If I can't be with him then I'll remember some of the wonderful times we've had together," she thought, and her mind went back to a day in Windsor Great Park when she had gone to watch him and some of the Royal family take part in a vigorously played polo game. The magnificence of the horses and the vitality and strength of the players had made it an exciting afternoon. Chris had played exceptionally well; he was an excellent horseman and had complete control of every situation. His smile had dazzled her each time he looked over at her. Diana remembered that afterward some of the players had asked about Margaret, his sister, who was in Europe on vacation. Diana wondered if she would approve of her brother wanting to marry an American. The impression she had received was that Margaret was one of the most forthright of the Drayton family—tenaciously protective of their heritage and, it would seem, rather difficult. From the photograph on the piano in the living room at the castle, she looked to be a very assured, beautifully dressed young woman, with a direct gaze that gave the impression she knew exactly what she wanted out of life. "It will be interesting to meet her one day," thought Diana.

She put her watch back eight hours to California time and began wondering what the next few days would hold. Relaxed now in her seat, she began to realize how tired she was. Perhaps the magazine would give her a few days before she would have to fly up to San Francisco. Diana had never actually worked with Ian before, except for the interview she had done on him, so this would be a very different experience in their relationship. He was a perfectionist in everything connected with his work; his enthusiasm for a project would mean his total and absolute attention to every detail. Lighting angles and composition were all part of his striving for excellence, and the critics had lauded his efforts.

After lunch and a movie that Diana could not concentrate on, she decided to try to sleep as the jet brought her closer and closer to Ian. She was disturbed once or twice by some noisy cardplayers as they snapped and shuffled their cards, laughing loudly, but soon even they were quiet and she found herself falling fast asleep. Several hours later she awoke with a start. Looking at her watch, she realized that the plane was now only an hour away from Los Angeles. Soon the enormous "meadow" of homes and freeways would come into view, and her vacation would be truly over.

Diana brushed her hair and freshened her

makeup, wondering all the time what she would say to Ian. Should she say outright what had happened, or slowly let him see that there was a change in her? She felt extremely agitated when she heard the flight attendant say over the intercom, "In preparing for our landing in Los Angeles, will all passengers please fasten their seat belts?"

Customs took forever, and finally her luggage was passed and stamped and she walked through the doors into the visitors' waiting area. She did not even have to look for Ian—he stood there towering above the crowd. His six-foot-four frame dominated everyone around him, and his suntanned face, dark curly hair, and moustache made him look like a typically relaxed, successful Californian.

His penetratingly blue eyes lit up when he saw Diana, and he pushed his way through the crowd and swept her up in his arms.

"Diana, how I've missed you!" Holding her at arm's length, he said admiringly, "You look great!"

He kissed her long and hard, and she reeled from the intensity of his greeting. The same elderly couple who had seen her impassioned farewell to Chris now stood in amazement and looked at each other, shaking their heads. "Such a hussy!" said the wife. The husband was still looking as she pulled his arm. "My, *my...*" he said again, only this time there was complete bewilderment.

Ian grabbed Diana's flight bag and guided her to the escalators, talking all the time. There was so much to tell her. First, the publishers were going to use her photograph on the cover of his book. Then there was the project in San Francisco, and he had a proposition to put to her about travel plans. Diana felt completely dazed. Pangs of guilt concerning Chris had already hit her, and she knew she was not responding too well. When they finally got her luggage, Ian left her for a few minutes to get his car. Diana stood outside the baggage entrance and watched people coming and going—some frantically running because of the fear of a missed plane, others casually waiting for a limousine or bus, and still others emotionally welcoming friends and families. She felt rather desolate. Ian had been so excited to see her and had been ecstatic about their trip to San Francisco, but she had hardly been able to say anything.

He pulled up in his red Porsche in front of her, jumped out, and put her luggage in the trunk. Then he opened the car door for her. As she leaned over to get into the car she saw that on the passenger seat was an exquisite bouquet of yellow roses—her favorite flowers.

"Oh, Ian, they're beautiful! Thank you." She turned to look at him and then started to cry.

"What in the world...? Since when do your beloved yellow roses make you cry?" He stood there completely mystified, not understanding what had made her break down like this.

"Forgive me. I'll tell you later." Diana took the flowers in her arms and sat down in the car. It was so typical of Ian to remember. Soon after they had first met they had walked past a florist shop; she had admired the roses in the window and he had immediately bought her an enormous bouquet. Since then he would often surprise her with them without any reason or anniversary. His thoughtfulness made it even more difficult for Diana to decide about the men in her life.

They drove out of the airport area in silence, and then Ian said, "Diana, I want to tell you what I think would be the most fabulous next two days for us."

"Ian, really I am absolutely exhausted from the flight. Could we wait for a while before discussing it?"

"Not really. You see, I have everything well in hand, and as a matter of fact we are right now on our way to San Francisco!"

Diana saw that he had turned onto the freeway in the opposite direction from her apartment and was heading north.

"Ian! This is ridiculous. I'm so tired, I need to adjust...I've been traveling for hours." After she saw that he was not paying any attention to her, she said pleadingly, "I have to go back to my apartment and get some other clothes."

"The clothes you have with you will be fine. England and San Francisco have about the same kind of weather." He drove on determinedly.

"I need to call the office and find out about the assignment."

"I already have. In fact I was there this morning, and they gave me this for you." He handed her a large envelope addressed to her.

By this time Diana was feeling thoroughly annoyed.

"Ian, since when do you run my life like this?" He had always been extremely dominant, but now even more so.

"As of now, and you're going to love it."

Angrily Diana threw the roses into the back of the car. Turning her back to him, she looked out the window. They drove on without talking for about five minutes, and after she was almost to the boiling point Diana said, through clenched teeth, "I need to get my mail and tell Sarah where I'll be."

Ian leaned over and opened the glove compartment, taking out a pile of letters. "Voila! I also went to your apartment and Sarah gave me your mail. She knows where you will be, so now what else do you need to do?"

Diana was so frustrated that she demanded that he stop at the nearest turnoff and go back to Los Angeles. Ian pretended he did not hear her and just drove on, singing "San Francisco" at the top of his voice, smiling infuriatingly the whole time.

A few minutes went by and he said, "Are you in a better mood now so we can talk?"

"Talk? I think you should have done that before you got on this highway—before you decided in your own presumptuous way to—"

"My, such long words! Preeesuuumptuuuuous! Must be the English influence."

IAN! You have got me so mad! Don't start making fun of the British or I'll—"

"You'll what?"

Diana realized that she had reacted too forcefully, so she looked straight ahead, watching the traffic coming in the opposite direction as it went on its way to Los Angeles.

"Diana, what happened in England? Since when are you so protective of our British cousins?"

She did not reply, but kept on watching the traffic. Chris's bracelet slid down her wrist and she hastily pushed it back under her sleeve. This was not the moment for Ian to see it.

"Well, if you're not going to talk to me, I'll listen to some good old Yankee music." He turned the radio on, and for the next half hour they drove on, the pounding of the music filling the car and making conversation impossible anyway.

As they approached San Luis Obispo, Ian turned off the highway and drove to a small restaurant. It didn't look too appetizing, but he felt it was time for coffee and perhaps a quiet peacemaking chat.

He got out of the car and came around to open the door for Diana. She just sat in stony silence, refusing to look at him.

"You know, this is so different from what I imagined our reunion would be. After a month I thought you would be so thrilled to see me that you'd be doing handstands over my Don Juan plans."

Diana still refused to speak.

"All right...listen, Diana. Well, at least look at me."

She turned to glare at him, her eyes flashing "Keep away from me" warnings.

"Let's have coffee and talk about this."

"That's what you should have done in the first place, instead of just taking over."

"Sorry, Mademoiselle Diana. I am a mad, impetuous man who is in love with a beautiful, but moody, young woman. The macho in me got carried away."

"Moody? Who's moody?" she shouted.

Ian lifted an eyebrow and smiled, and Diana,

in spite of herself, began to laugh.

"All right, I'll have some coffee and we'll TALK about these incredible plans of yours."

She got out of the car and reached over to take the roses, laying them on the front seat. "Sorry," she whispered.

Over coffee they reached a truce. If Ian would quietly explain and ask her opinion about the next few days' arrangements, she would listen and acquiesce if they seemed agreeable.

"Diana, the only reason I took this assignment was so I could be with you. You don't seem to realize how much I've missed you." Diana was silent. "Well, we're spending the night in Carmel at the Pine Cone Inn. Remember, we stopped there once for brunch?" She nodded. "Then, after you've caught up on some sleep, we can leisurely make our way to the Hyatt in San Francisco."

"Do you realize that to me the time is now four o'clock in the morning? I am really dead tired, Ian. Carmel means at least several more hours' drive."

"You can sleep all the way there. The inn is expecting a late arrival, so why don't you just relax and enjoy your return to America?"

Jet lag had truly set in for Diana, and she was so exhausted that she felt it was useless to object anymore. The drive back to Los Angeles would be just as tiring as going on to Carmel, so she resigned herself to accepting Ian's arrangements.

Diana had never seen Ian so elated before. He seemed so much more carefree than she had ever known him, and the joy of seeing her after a month away had melted the edges of his usually kind but austere manner. He was incredibly hand-some in a rugged way, and being near him again had begun to bring back the old feelings she had for him. She was in a daze. It seemed as if the episode with Chris in England was just a dream, and as if she had now awakened to find herself back in California with this man whom she knew so well and of whom she was extremely fond. While Ian drove on, as the sun was setting over the broad, rolling hills, Diana fell asleep. She awakened several hours later to Ian's gentle tugging at her sleeve.

"Wake up, beautiful one. We're here. Carmel awaits you."

She rubbed her eyes and at first could not imagine where she was. Then, as she looked around and saw the lamplight illuminating the Pine Cone Inn sign, she realized they were in Carmel. The beauty of this small but beautifully decorated Victorian-style hotel had delighted them the last time they had been here, and they had promised themselves they would return for a long weekend sometime.

A fire was burning in the fireplace in the lobby, and as Ian checked them in, Diana stood watching the flames dance around the huge logs. The nights in Carmel reminded her of English summer nights, misty and sometimes in need of a fire. She felt a pang of homesickness for the castle...then Ian was beside her, and as he kissed her on the ear he whispered, "They've given us a suite." When Diana turned to protest, he said immediately, "They didn't have two separate rooms."

"Is this what you requested, Ian? A suite? I mean, when you made the reservations?"

They had argued many times about Diana's refusal to sleep with him, but he had always told her finally that she was worth waiting for—he wanted her to be his wife. He had laughed at her old-fashioned standards and had stated she must be the last virgin in California.

Ian did not answer Diana's question about the suite, but told the porter to take their luggage up and they would follow shortly. Sitting by the fire, Diana spoke quietly but firmly to Ian.

"We've been through this so many times," she said wearily.

"Diana, I haven't seen you for over a month... don't you think I have any feelings?"

"Of course, but you know exactly how *I* feel."

"Look, Diana, the suite has a bed in each room. I promise I will stay in my quarters if you would kindly stop making a fuss. So let's go there and you can sleep to your heart's content."

Diana reluctantly followed him up the winding staircase, wondering if she were really awake or still sleeping in the four-poster bed at Drayton Castle.

The door to the suite was open and their luggage had been left in the living room. Ian took her suitcases into the bedroom and deliberately set them down by the old Victorian brass bed. He came back in the living room and walked over to the sofa bed.

"See, here's a bed for me," and he pulled it out, throwing the cushions in all directions. "Satisfied?" His voice had taken on a very weary and dejected tone.

Diana went into the bedroom and began to unpack one of her suitcases. The magazine, which contained the red rose that Chris had given her, was the first thing she saw, and in her sleepiness she tossed it onto a chair, not noticing that the rose fell to the floor. As she got ready for bed she looked at Chris's bracelet and decided to keep it in her handbag—she could not explain everything to Ian right now. The yellow roses that Ian had given her were put in the bathroom sink, and as she filled it with water she thought how well the flowers had stood up to her fit of temper.

As she switched the light off by her bed, she

felt so confused. Lying in the big brass bed with its old-fashioned white-lace comforter, she thought of all that had happened to her. How was she going to tell Ian? He tapped on her door, and in the light from the lamp post outside the window, Diana saw him standing there dejectedly.

"May I at least have a good-night kiss?" She nodded and he came over to sit on the bed.

"Something has happened to you, Diana. What is it?"

"Could we please talk in the morning?" Right now she couldn't face all that telling him about Chris would entail.

"All right...sleep well, my beautiful Diana." He touched her hair as he bent to kiss her tenderly on the lips. "It's so good to have you back. Please, no more month-long vacations without me again."

As he got up to leave he saw the rose on the floor. Picking it up, he looked at it for a moment, then said questioningly, "From an admirer perhaps?" and put it on the nightstand. Walking to the door, he whispered, "Yes, Diana, I think you have a great deal to tell me."

He closed the door and lay down on the sofa, his mind racing—thinking of the way she had seemed so distant. It surely was not just because of jet lag. The rose nagged at him. Suddenly he was remembering another scene when he was only

22 and his fiancee had told him she was marrying another man whom she had met while he had been serving in Vietnam. Angrily he had lashed out at her, vowing that he would never trust another woman in his life. It had been a destructive episode and had taken years for the scars to heal. But the doubts that were now racing through him were breaking the old wounds open again. He punched his pillow, trying to get comfortable, but sleep would not come easily to him that night. He had never wanted anything so much in all his life as to be married to Diana. His career, which had meant everything to him, had taken second place compared with her. Was he now going to be desperately hurt once again?

The telephone rang—the sound bringing him back to the loneliness of the room. He reached out to answer it at the same time Diana picked up the extension in the bedroom. Almost simultaneously they both said, "Hello?"

There was a long pause, filled by the rushing sound of the overseas cable, then a man's voice said, "Diana, is that you?"

Quietly Ian put down the telephone...his fears were now becoming a reality.

Chapter Six

Diana sat up in bed, trying desperately to get wide awake. The sound of Chris's voice with Ian only next door had confused her. Had Chris heard Ian's voice? What was Ian thinking? Somehow she tried to sound normal as she said, "Oh, Chris, how good to hear from you."

Chris had heard a man's voice answer the phone as well as Diana's, and he was completely confused. "Diana, who was that that answered?" Then a thought hit him. "Was it Ian?"

Diana didn't want to have to explain the circumstances. She knew that the more she said the worse it would sound.

"Yes, it was."

Before she had any time to say more, Chris said in a hurt, angry voice, "Sorry for interrupting," and hung up.

Disheartened, Diana put the phone down, knowing what he must be thinking. She looked at her watch. It was now 2 A.M., so it would be 10 A.M. in England. He would know that it was practically the middle of the night when he called her. She buried her face in her hands, tears now forming as she realized what he must be thinking.

She tossed in bed, unable to sleep. Ian was probably awake too, wondering who was calling her from overseas. Finally she got up about 5 A.M., went over to the window, and looked out at the deserted street below. The light from the lamp post cast a warm glow over the pine trees as they swayed in the breeze coming from the sea. She dressed quietly in her jeans, threw on a sweater, and opened her door as softly as possible, hoping that Ian was asleep. Then, seeing that he seemed to be sleeping, she opened the door of the suite and left the inn to walk and think on the beach.

She had walked here before with Ian and they had enjoyed the invigorating sea air and the sound of the gulls. Laughing, they had raced along the beach, throwing pebbles in the azure sea. But now she walked alone, and everything looked so different to her. The sun was just beginning to rise, but in the half-light the cypress trees took on a menacing look and the sea, as it pounded against the rocks, was gray and bleak.

Diana sat down under one of the gaunt trees and, with her knees drawn up under her chin, looked out at the blustery scene. The gulls were beginning their furtive hunt for food, and she watched as they found shells and dashed them against the rocks, breaking them and pouncing on their edible trophies with delight. She felt like one of their prey—as if she had been attacked and left broken. How could everything have changed so quickly?

"Chris must have called my apartment and Sarah must have given him the number of the inn," she thought. Anger welled within her as she thought of the way Ian had now put her in a compromising situation. She should not have shared the suite even though she had been so tired.

Drifts of fog moved in from the sea, enveloping her like a shroud, and she shivered as the dampness seemed to seep into her body. She decided to walk the whole of the curved mile-long beach, since the alternative—facing Ian—did not appeal to her. The foaming breakers swirled near her feet as she faced the wind and strode on, unaware that Ian was watching her from the roadway.

He called her name several times, but the wind swept his voice away and Diana kept walking. Ian started to run toward her, still calling her name, and as she turned he waved. She knew she had to face him—there was no putting off all they had to talk about. Walking back to him, she noticed that he was wearing the white Irish sweater she had given him last Christmas. The contrast with his dark hair seemed to accentuate the color of his eyes and suntan.

"Are you warm enough, Diana? It's so damp." He put his arm around her protectively as they walked together along the white sand.

Diana had not expected this reaction from Ian. She had seen him furious at times when things did not please him, and she thought that this would have been the situation now.

"Well, that was a very short phone call last night, Diana."

"Yes, it was." She looked at him, trying to decide what he was thinking. "It was from England."

"I gathered that."

"I tried to tell you yesterday, Ian, that I had met someone over there."

"I'm sure you met many people over there, Diana. What was this...what they call a 'shipboard romance'? Everything always looks very attractive when you're far from home. Did he 'sweep you off your feet,' as they say?"

Diana had to be truthful. "Yes, Ian, he did. I hate to have to tell you this. I don't ever want to hurt you in any way. But I—"

"Diana, I knew something had happened. I was just waiting for you to tell me." He kicked a shell into the sea, the determination on his face showing his deep concern. But he went on, lightheartedly: "I chalk it up to experience. Never have had much luck with women..."

"That's ridiculous, Ian. You know girls are crazy about you."

"Oh, yes, for a while, then something always happens."

Diana turned to him, her anger leaving as she saw the hurt in his eyes. He had put her in a compromising situation, but she was as much at fault as he was.

"Ian, I never imagined something like this would happen to me. When I said good-bye to you as I left for England, meeting someone else was the last thing on my mind." She brushed the hair from her eyes. "Then at Aunt Janet's one night I met Chris Drayton and something just seemed to happen between us. He invited me to his home in the country."

Ian stopped walking. "Oh, really? Does he have a little cottage for two? I suppose he wanted to show you his etchings, as they say in bonnie old England?" His tone was now extremely sarcastic and his mood was changing rapidly.

"No, he doesn't have a cottage...he lives in a castle. His mother and father are titled and he is the heir!" flashed Diana, now on the defensive.

"Well, no wonder he seemed so attractive. All that money, prestige, *and* a castle. How could you resist, Diana?" Then, thinking of what might have happened between them, he said, "Or did you?"

"Ian, you know how I feel about that...of course not. I really like him for himself and not because he happens to be from a prominent family. But, thanks to you, now he probably never wants to see me again."

"What do you mean, 'thanks to me'?"

"Getting that suite last night—he heard your voice on the phone and now I know he thinks the worst."

"I hope he does. Diana, does our relationship of over a year mean absolutely nothing to you? I thought we were going to be married."

"You knew I wasn't sure, Ian."

Ignoring her, he went on. "I must not have been a very important part of your life, if you can suddenly meet a titled foreigner and just like that decide you've had enough of me."

"Ian, you've got it all wrong. I've never prayed so much about anything. I still care for you very deeply and this has been one of the most difficult situations I have ever faced. I don't want to hurt either of you."

"Well, it's too late for that. I feel as if I've been hit by one of those rocks out there."

They continued to walk, and now the sun was shining hazily through the fog. Carmel was coming alive as various tradesmen began their deliveries and cars started to drive down Ocean Avenue. The small restaurants were opening for breakfast.

"Well, Diana Lewis, no matter what you think, I'm not giving up that easily to any rival. You can pine all you want for him, but this Englishman—who probably has quite a name among the giggly debutantes—will not change my love for you. It was possibly just a passing phase on his part, Diana."

She remembered Aunt Janet's warning about how many hearts Chris had broken. But she also recalled how sincere he seemed, how very much in love with her.

Ian continued, "Diana, I refuse to lose my appetite over this brief British encounter." He bent to kiss her, then dragged her by the hand and raced toward the town.

"Breakfast calls, broken romances or not!"

They found a small cafe that specialized in lingonberry pancakes, and to her surprise Diana ate heartily, despite the fact that she was still so concerned about Chris. She had to talk to him and explain the circumstances of last night.

Chapter Seven

After breakfast, Diana returned to the hotel on Ocean Avenue to pack, since they were leaving for San Francisco that morning. Ian walked back to the beach to take some photographs of the wild and beautiful scene. He never seemed to tire of Carmel's rugged, haunting beauty.

As she entered the suite, Diana wondered if she should try to call Chris. There were probably at least ten minutes before Ian would return from the beach, and she had to try to explain to Chris what had happened. She dialed the overseas operator. While she was waiting for the call to go through, she looked over at the rose that Chris had given her only the morning before. It seemed like days had passed. Diana heard the sound of a telephone being picked up and the butler's voice answering.

"Drayton Castle."

"Edwards, this is Diana Lewis calling from California. Is Lord Christopher there?"

"I'm sorry, Miss Diana, he left this morning for London. He did not say whether he was going to be staying at the family residence or not."

"Could you please let me have the telephone number there?"

"Certainly, miss."

Diana wrote it down and thanked Edwards. She dialed the overseas operator once more and asked for the London number, but even as it started to ring the sound of Ian returning made her put down the receiver. She would have to wait until she got to the hotel in San Francisco.

The journey was filled with tension between Ian and Diana. Checking out of the Pine Cone Inn, he had noticed a charge for a call to England. This infuriated him, and after questioning Diana about it, he drove in silence.

Diana took the opportunity to read her mail; she had completely forgotten about it last night, and now she saw that there was a letter postmarked New York. It was from her brother James:

Dear Diana:

By the time you read this, I will be into rehearsals for a revival of "A Man for All Seasons." It is hard to believe and I am still reeling from all that has happened. Diana, it's a great showcase for me and my agent really feels I can go places through it. Apart from all that, I am overjoyed to be in a play like "Seasons" because it has such a wonderful message.

I've been rambling on about myself and not asking how you are. Did you have a good vacation? Thanks for your card. What a fantastic place to stay! Castle Drayton looks like something out of a medieval movie! Any chance I can get an invite too someday?

Diana, you *have* to come to the opening night. It's going to be at the Morosco Theater on September 18th. Can you swing it with your crusty editor? Tell him it's the most important night of your brother's life.

Call me soon and let me know. I rehearse

all day, but am usually back at my apartment by 10 P.M.

Love you, dear sis,
James

"How wonderful!"

For a moment, Diana had forgotten the tension in the car while she read James's letter.

Ian, his eyes on the road and his chin set determinedly, said, "And what is so wonderful?"

"James has landed a part on Broadway in 'A
Man for All Seasons.' I'm so delighted for him.
It will mean so much to his career."

"Great. I'm glad someone is having some good
luck." Then he added, "He deserves it—he's a
good actor."

Diana turned to Ian gratefully. "He really is.
I'm so proud of him. He wants me to go to his
opening night. I hope I can get off after being
away so long."

"Somehow you usually manage to get what you
want, Diana." Ian's tone made her aware once
more of their conflict. She looked quickly at him
and decided to ignore that remark. Instead, she
opened a large envelope that Ian had brought
from her office.

Engrossing herself in the San Francisco assignment, she became acquainted with the history of
the mansion they would be covering. It had be-
longed to the Gary family and had just been com-

pletely redecorated; it was soon to be opened to the public. The Garys had been a prominent San Francisco family, and with the death of the last of the Garys the mansion had been willed to the city. There had been a great deal of publicity about the opening, and now Diana was to write an in-depth article covering the family and the events that had taken place there, and describing the architecture and authentic period furniture, which had been brought from all over the country by the renowned interior decorator, Irene Shannon. As Diana read on, she wondered what Ms. Shannon was like. Easily intimidated by successful career women, yet being able to give an air of complete assurance, Diana made a mental note not to be disconcerted by this very wealthy woman.

They arrived in San Francisco, and as always the city made Diana thrill to its magnificent skyline. The sun shining on the myriad of windows in the skyscrapers, the steep hills, the architecturally magnificent bridges teeming with endless streams of cars, the unsurpassed beauty of the Pacific Ocean—all contributed to San Francisco's reputation as one of the most picturesque cities in America.

As they drove up to the entrance of the Hyatt Regency Hotel, Diana wondered if there would be another argument about their rooms. Ian did not even look at her as he got out of the car, and after the luggage was taken by the porter he strode ahead of her to the reception desk. "Two *singles,* please, for Ms. Diana Lewis and Mr. Ian Kingsley." Diana pretended to ignore the sarcastic tone and looked up at the vastness of the Hyatt's interior. The open lobby extended for almost a city block and contained shops, restaurants and lounges, surrounded by balconies from each floor of the starkly modern hotel. A piano was playing, and the music wafted above the sound of fountains and the murmur of conversation which emanated from those casually sitting, listening, and relaxing.

Ian came over to Diana and with great ceremony reached for her hand and placed a room key in it. "Sorry, I'm next door to you. Tried to get another floor, but they're fully booked."

"Ian, please, let's not go on like this. Let's at least try to enjoy our stay here."

"I intend to," he stated loftily, and walked over to the elevator. Diana followed, wondering just how these next few days were going to turn out. "I *have* to concentrate on this article," she thought. As the elevator ascended to the thirtieth floor, Ian read a message that had been left for him at the reception desk.

"Irene Shannon would like to dine with us this evening. Are you free?"

"Of course I am, Ian."

"All right, I'll call her and let you know what time."

Diana opened the door of her room, and as she heard Ian's door slam she suddenly felt desperately alone. She had never minded staying at hotels before, but now somehow the modern furnishings of the room seemed to stress her loneliness. The porter had left her luggage, but before unpacking she walked over to the window and looked out on the breathtaking view. The sun was beginning to go down, and its warm light cast shadows, making the skyline take on a new aspect. Lights were going on in the countless windows, and soon the city would be illuminated like a backdrop for a Broadway play.

Her thoughts turned to her brother James in New York. How she wished he were here! She desperately needed someone to talk to—someone who would understand all that had happened to her during these last few weeks. Diana remembered how James had always been a sympathetic listener as they were growing up. The scene of their parents' fatal air crash came to her mind as she saw a plane flying high above the skyline, and she thought of the day when James and she had cried together at their loss. His arms had enfolded her like a warm blanket of comfort—how she needed them now!

The telephone rang, interrupting her thoughts. It was Ian. "Seven-thirty all right with you? We're going to eat here."

"That will be fine, Ian. Thanks." Diana put down the telephone and immediately began to wonder what she would wear. Her clothing had not been hung up for nearly two days. She hastily unpacked and found a dress that didn't have too many wrinkles. Trying it on, she looked critically at herself in the mirror. Fortunately the dress was one that she always felt confident in. She glanced at her watch—only 45 minutes to do something with her hair and put on new makeup.

She took one last look in the mirror before joining Ian and felt reasonably pleased with her appearance. Now to face Irene Shannon.

As the elevator opened at the lobby, Diana saw Ian talking to the famed decorator, who was dressed in a black suit that spoke volumes. It was obviously not bought off the rack—not even the rack of an expensive store. It was definitely couturier. Her jewelry was not opulent, but it told the world that the wearer was rich—very rich. She was San Francisco chic, with a great sense of style.

Hesitantly Diana walked toward them, and Ian, after a few more seconds of conversation, introduced her to Irene. As Diana looked into this sophisticated woman's eyes, Irene returned her gaze and the two women took an instant dislike of each other. Irene, with her black, shiny hair pulled back into an immaculate knot, made Diana feel immediately inferior. The wrinkles in her dress seemed accentuated and she was more than conscious of the fact that her hair had been a last-minute effort.

As they were led to their table by the maitre d', Diana had the apprehensive feeling that this would not be the most pleasant of meals. It was obvious from the start that Ian was going to ignore Diana as much as possible and be very attentive to Irene.

"I've heard so much about you, Ian, and admired your work for quite a while. The Gary Mansion is very privileged in having you cover it. I have to be honest and say that this meeting has been one I've been looking forward to tremendously." Irene's high-bred accent lingered over every word as she gazed at Ian. She had already acquired and divorced two husbands, each of them extremely wealthy. Now she was obviously enjoying her freedom. As the meal progressed, she flirted outrageously with Ian. Diana found that each time she tried to enter the conversation she was either interrupted or ignored, and Ian and Irene's attitude made her feel that anything she could add to the conversation would be inconsequential.

"The Gary Mansion people are expecting us at

9 A.M. tomorrow, and everything has been cleared for you to start shooting in whatever rooms you feel will best portray the mansion's style, Ian," Irene purred.

Diana remarked, "It really sounds like a fabulous project. I'm looking forward to getting started on it."

"Oh, yes," Irene turned to her patronizingly, "you're doing a little article on the house, aren't you?"

"It's going to be the cover story, so it won't be *too* insignificant." Ian sensed the feeling that Diana had put into those words and looked from woman to woman, intrigued by the prospect of the results of their close proximity over the next couple of days.

"Of course, the photographs in a project like this are really the most important statement that can be made. Photography makes everything come alive—that is, the photography of such high caliber as Ian Kingsley's." Irene smiled at him ingratiatingly.

Ian smiled back, flattered by the acceptance of his work by this discerning and beautiful woman.

'If you will excuse me," Diana interrupted Ian's moment of glory, "I really am still on English time and am very tired. I think I will skip dessert tonight and get to bed early, so I will be in good shape for tomorrow." She rose from the table, and with a quick "good night" to both of them she left the restaurant before Ian could see the hurt and the tears that were now beginning to form.

Once in her room, she flung her handbag on the bed and threw off her shoes. Diana wanted to cry, but she brushed away the tears and refused to yield to the luxury. "My eyes will be swollen in the morning, and I'm not going to let that woman make me look like a cub reporter at a school benefit. Oh, she makes me so angry!"

Diana took off her earrings and was about to throw those down when she remembered that they had been a gift from James. She wondered if she should call him. Looking at her watch, she realized it would be 2 A.M. in New York. Her thoughts turned to Chris, and quickly she calculated what the time would be in London: 6 A.M. It was too early to call him. Frustrated, she switched on the television and watched the news as she got ready for bed.

The stainless steel accents and modern paintings in her room made her feel eons away from Drayton Castle and Chris. The newscaster droned on in the background of her thoughts, and she finally turned the television off and set her alarm for 6 A.M. She would call Chris before she left for the Gary Mansion, hoping that he would be home.

Sinking gratefully into the soft beige sheets,

Diana read through the material on the mansion once more, then leaned over and switched off the light. But sleep evaded her, even though she was so tired. Her mind was racing with all the conversation at dinner and Ian's obvious enjoyment at being fawned over by that woman. Angrily she turned and looked at the magnificent scene from her window. She wondered if Ian were still talking to Irene Shannon. Diana looked at the alarm clock—it was 1 A.M. and she still had not heard him go into his room. Finally, at about 1:30 A.M., she was almost drifting off to sleep when she heard his door slam. He had had quite a long conversation with Irene. "Business, of course," thought Diana, "but what *kind* of business?" She was angry with herself that it even bothered her. If she really loved Chris, why should she resent Ian finding someone else? It would make it all so much simpler for her. Yet she knew that Irene's attention to Ian had not only struck deep at her pride, but that she also had feelings that were still very real for him. No one had stirred up such angry emotions in Diana before. Was it jealousy?

"Yes, Lord, forgive me. Please show me what I should do. I feel very lost at this moment. And please forgive me for wanting to dig my nails into Irene Shannon's beautifully made-up face!"

Chapter Eight

The alarm clock's piercing beeps brought Diana out of a deep but fretful sleep. She looked at the time, then lay back on the pillow, remembering that today would be extremely difficult. Her feelings must not show as she dealt with Irene's deceptively innocent provocations. Lying there, she thought that Irene was basically the type of woman that Ian had always had little time for—sophisticated, highly successful, always one jump ahead of any man, and one who knew exactly what she wanted not only out of life but also out of a man. Diana had hurt Ian deeply when she had told him about Chris, and now he was retaliating—trying to hurt her. Or did he really find Irene that attractive?

As Diana dressed, her mind was on looking her very best. She brushed her lustrous blonde hair over and over again, finally delighted with the way it looked. Her makeup glided on, and the night's sleep had restored her, making the intense blue eyes and soft, flawless, porcelain-like skin radiate a beauty that even the seemingly assured Ms. Shannon would find disconcertingly competitive. Diana dressed in her navy suit and white georgette blouse.

Feeling confident, Diana dialed Chris's London number. "Please let him be there," she prayed, and then as the housekeeper's voice answered she was rewarded to hear, "Yes, Lord Christopher is in. May I say who's calling?" Diana waited for what seemed an eternity, then Chris picked up an extension and said, "Hello." His voice sounded distant, not like the warm, wonderful Chris she had become so deeply attached to in such a short time.

"Oh, Chris, I'm so thankful to have found you in. I'm so sorry about the other night. Goodness knows what you must have been thinking."

"About what?"

"Well, you really got the wrong impression. Ian had planned a trip to San Francisco for the article I was assigned. He's doing the photography..." Diana tried to explain about the suite to Chris, but there was a long pause. "Chris, he answered the phone in the living room—please believe me."

"Of course." There was a matter-of-fact attitude and a feeling of almost not caring.

"Chris, I really do care for you and miss you so much. I had to call and tell you before I left for the mansion."

"I see, Diana. Well, I've had two very rough days and I find it hard to understand just what is going on. It's given me time to think about 'us,' and maybe I was rather hasty. I really don't know anymore."

"Chris, how could you have changed so quickly? Don't you have any faith in me?"

"Yes, but not too much in myself. I went out last night and got completely bombed...visited some old friends and lived it up for a night." There was a long pause. "Sorry, I don't know what else to say."

The rushing sound of the overseas cable seemed

to overtake their thoughts, and Diana realized that there *was* nothing else to say.

"Chris, I'll write you soon. Perhaps by then we will both be in a different frame of mind."

"I hope so, Diana. I feel as if a British Railways train has run over me...I'm not sure whether it's the hangover or the shock of Ian."

"Please, Chris, try to understand. I've prayed so much about us and about him..." Her voice trailed off and she managed to whisper, "Good-bye."

"Good-bye, Diana." His voice repeated the words parrot-fashion and then he was gone. Diana knew how much he must have been in pain to have gone off with his friends like that. He had once told her he wanted to forget that kind of life and now live "completely for my lovely Diana."

The telephone rang intrusively, making Diana come back to the concerns of the day.

"Diana, where are you? We'll be late if you don't hurry." Ian's voice sounded very agitated.

"Sorry, I'm almost ready. Meet you in the lobby in two minutes."

Diana felt as if she were in shock from her talk with Chris, but managed to gather together her handbag, notebook, and all the material she would need. Ian was waiting in the lobby, his photography equipment surrounding him.

"Can't be late for Irene. Her time is very

valuable. I've got to set up my lights." He looked at her still annoyed, but very much aware of how beautiful she looked.

"I am *not* late, Ian. I haven't even had breakfast yet."

"Too bad. You shouldn't make so many phone calls. Your phone has been busy for ages."

She glared at him and looked at the clock in the lobby. "I have at least 45 minutes before I have to leave. Go on without me. Ms. Shannon will be ecstatic."

Diana was dealing with a host of emotions, and now the temptation to be catty was taking over. "You don't need me to start setting up your lights. Irene can run around and plug in whatever needs plugging in!"

She turned and walked directly over to the coffee shop, leaving Ian to battle his way through the revolving doors with his equipment—angrier than ever. Diana ordered a large breakfast, which when it arrived she could not eat. She was angry with Chris, with Ian, and of course with Ms. Shannon. Mostly she was angry with herself for not being able to control her emotions. After coffee she felt more in command of herself and took a taxi over to the mansion.

It was a glorious morning, and the traffic that filled the streets and the excitement of being in San Francisco made her forget, for a while, all that had transpired. As the taxi drove up Nob Hill, the beauty of the pre-earthquake architecture of the mansion intrigued Diana, and already in her mind she was "writing" the article about the "ostentatious, white-painted, redwood, clapboard home that had escaped the fire and earthquake of 1906." After paying the taxi driver she turned and looked up admiringly at this fine late-Victorian splendor with delight. It was haughty, yet magnificent. Its curlicues, brackets, carvings, balconies, and imposing turrets seemed to dare the passerby to take it for granted.

Diana ran up the impressive steps leading to the ornate front door and rang the bell with great deliberation. A few moments later Irene Shannon, dressed in a dynamic red silk Halston suit and large black straw picture hat, opened the door. Her irritation when she saw that it was Diana was obvious.

"You really have interrupted a most important shot, Diana." Turning on her high-heeled, black patent leather shoes, she walked briskly through the oak-paneled entrance hall and disappeared into one of the large reception rooms.

Diana ignored her and began exploring the mansion on her own. In the taxi Diana had decided to leave Ian to the wiles of Irene, and that only when it was absolutely necessary would Diana encounter her. She picked up one of the illustrated brochures from the antique hall table and proceeded to give herself a tour.

As Diana went through the dark-yet-vibrant entrance hall, with the light shining through the Victorian stained-glass front door, she thought begrudgingly, "Irene has really done a fantastic job. Excelled herself." The feeling of the 1880s, the Gold Rush era, came alive through the subtly placed furnishings. It was not one of Diana's favorite periods as far as furniture was concerned—too ornate and overpowering—yet there was a certain quality about the whole house that made her imagine a family living there during those times.

Climbing the wide, grand staircase, Diana explored upstairs and finally came to her favorite room. Irene had decorated it in white wicker in contrast to the heavy dark furniture and copies of the authentic dark red wallpapers of the other rooms. This room was done in pastels, gauzelike draperies, and masses of ferns.

Diana was taking in the beauty of it all when she heard footsteps behind her.

"Miss Lewis?"

Standing there was a distinguished-looking man dressed in a dark gray tailored suit.

"How do you do. I am John Clements, trustee and director of the Gary Mansion Project. It is a pleasure to meet you."

As Diana shook hands with him, she thought how well he went with the mansion. He seemed to have stepped out of the past.

"We are delighted that you are doing a cover story for your magazine, and I want you to know that we are only too happy to help in any way."

"Thank you, Mr. Clements." Looking around the room again, she said, "Tell me, what was this room used for?"

"Well, the first Mrs. Gary used it to sew and relax in. They had a large family, so she took pleasure in being able to come up here and get away from the stress of running a house of such considerable size."

It was obvious to Diana that John Clements found her attractive; he walked closely to her as he pointed out the different items of interest. She was relieved when she heard Ian's voice calling to her. Excusing herself, she went out to the landing to answer him.

"Diana, we are due to go upstairs now. Do you want Irene to cue you in on anything down here?"

She ran down the stairs and entered the main reception room. It was a large sunken room, with Oriental carpets and a large, ornate fireplace. The walls were paneled in rich, warm-toned Honduras mahogany. Two chandeliers dominated the room as they hung suspended from the highly decorated ceilings.

"Oh, Ian, I'm sure Diana only has to write a few sentences about this room. Your photography will say everything that is needed." Irene gathered up her handbag and coat and walked haughtily toward the two steps leading up to the wide double doors. As she reached the top step her heel caught in one of the wires leading to Ian's lights and she tripped and fell down, landing sideways on her right ankle. With a scream of pain that could have been heard over the Golden Gate Bridge, she sat in a crumpled heap, spewing volumes and blaming Ian for leaving the wire in her path.

John Clements rushed to her side and proceeded to calm her, assuring her that he would take her immediately to his doctor, who was close by. Picking her up in his arms, he made a grand exit through the doors with Ian running after him.

Diana stood in the middle of the room with very mixed feelings. She was sorry that Irene had been injured, but delighted that Ian had seen her true colors. When he returned from seeing her into John Clements' car, he looked almost relieved himself.

"Do you think she'll sue me?"

"Who knows? With someone like Irene *anything* is possible."

"She has driven me absolutely crazy...I'm sorry she had to get hurt, but I'm relieved I can continue without her breathing down my neck.''

Diana laughed. "Those are my sentiments completely.'' Turning to him she said, "Come and see the upstairs...it really is quite a house, and I have lots of great ideas as to how I'm going to cover it. Imagine the parties this house must have seen, the families who have lived and loved here!''

Together they walked up the curved staircase, laughing and enjoying the peace even though there was a sense of guilt at the cause of it.

As they explored the rooms, Diana sensed that Ian was more interested in her than in the furnishings. In the master bedroom he took her in his arms and whispered, "Sorry I've been such a bear. Jealousy does not become me.'' Kissing her gently, he suddenly put her at arm's length and said mockingly, "But then neither does it suit you, Miss Lewis. You must admit that you have been very jealous of the incomparable Irene Shannon.''

"I do admit it, but I also admit that I find her one of the most obnoxious women I've ever met. If you ever find me becoming like her, *please tell me!*'' They laughed together and Ian kissed her once more, only this time it was anything but gentle.

Diana realized that things might be getting out of hand and pushed him away. "Ian, to work...to work. We still have a great deal to cover.''

Ian brushed his moustache with his fingers and looked at her, longing to be able to take her in his arms again. But he too realized that there was an enormous amount of work ahead of them. Changing gears mentally, he went from room to room, deciding which ones would lend themselves best to his photography.

He called to Diana, "Let's work as late as we can and finish tonight, so we can get an early start back to Los Angeles in the morning."

"Good idea," called Diana, finding that the mood of desolation that she had felt earlier was now changing. She was determined to enjoy the next few hours in San Francisco, so she put at the back of her mind the disturbing phone call to Chris.

"I know a great little restaurant overlooking the bay at Fisherman's Wharf," shouted Ian as he went down the staircase to gather up his equipment.

"Wonderful! I'm ravenous for clam chowder and crab!" responded Diana as she went back to her notebook, concentrating completely on her article. The day had started out very depressingly, but now she felt as if the future would take care of itself.

Chapter Nine

❦

As Diana kissed Ian good night at the door of her apartment, she thought of how wonderful their drive home had been. They had sung songs and he had been in his best of moods, making her laugh at different reminiscences they had shared. With a promise to call him tomorrow, she shut the door and turned to look at her apartment. It had been such a long time since seeing it that the furniture and surroundings seemed to welcome her.

Calling out to Sarah, her roommate, she walked through the apartment looking for her. Lights had been left on all over the place, but there was no sign of Sarah. In the kitchen were notes stuck on the refrigerator that Sarah had written, mainly to herself.

"DON'T EAT UNLESS ABSOLUTELY NECESSARY TO YOUR HEALTH." "GO AWAY AND THINK ABOUT THESE EXTRA MOUTHFULS." There were photographs of herself: "NOT ONE EXTRA POUND OR YOU ARE TOMORROW'S UNEMPLOYED MODEL."

Diana opened the refrigerator and laughed. Sarah needn't worry—there was nothing there but a dried piece of cheese and some nonfat milk that had passed its expiration date. A lone apple graced the fruit bin. Shutting the door, Diana found a note on the kitchen table:

> Diana—WELCOME HOME—sorry I'm not here to greet you, but am going to Santa Barbara to do a cover for *Women's Day.* Imagine! Am so afraid I will be too fat by the time I get there, and they'll fire me. See you soon—Love, Sarah.

"I'm so glad I'm not a model," thought Diana

as she walked through the living room to her bedroom, eating the solitary apple. It was so good to see her own familiar things. So much had happened during these last weeks, but now she could relax, unpack, sort out her wardrobe, and take it easy. Then she remembered the article on the Gary Mansion. Her editor, Tom Bartlett, would want it "like yesterday" as soon as he knew she was back in town, and he would be hounding her. Tonight, however, she would take a long, hot bath and forget everything.

In an old, comfortable robe and with her hair wrapped in a towel, Diana sat down on her bed and began to sort through her suitcases. At the bottom of one she found a carefully wrapped package and realized that it was the cup and saucer that Chris had bought for her the day they had tea in Drayton Village. Could he really have changed his mind about her? Sadly, she took the cup and saucer out to the kitchen and put them on the table. Then, quickly, she put them away in one of the cupboards.

"I don't want to wake up to unhappy reminders," she thought, turning off the kitchen light and returning to her bedroom. Deliberately, she went to her handbag and took out the beautiful gold bracelet. She read the inscription, "To Diana—Forever, Chris."

"Not too much 'forever' about this romance,"

she whispered, and hid it at the bottom of her lingerie drawer, as if to say, "Out of sight, out of mind."

In the loneliness of her apartment, Diana shed the tears that she had kept back in San Francisco. She had believed that Chris really loved her. Perhaps Ian was right after all: It had just been a "shipboard romance"—nothing lasting.

Diana opened the drawer of her bedside table and found the small white New Testament that her mother and father had given to her when she had been confirmed at their church. On the flyleaf was written, "For our daughter Diana, with our love and prayers that He will always be first in your life. Mother and Dad." Turning to the back, where the psalms were, Diana read a verse from Psalm 34. It seemed to speak to her in a new and comforting way:

> The Lord is nigh unto them that are of a broken heart, and saveth such as be of a contrite spirit.

Diana found herself praying, "Thank You, Lord, for being near me, even when I have forgotten You so many times. Guide me and forgive me for not putting You first. I seem to find so much that is more important. Be with Chris tonight, wherever he is. And bless Ian."

Burying her face in the pillow, she let her tears

flow, feeling consolation as they poured out. Then
the telephone started ringing. Should she ignore
it? Just let it ring? Her voice would give away
the fact that she had been crying. Wiping away
her tears, she sat up and decided to answer it.
Clearing her voice, she managed a clear and strong
"Hello?"

"Diana, how great to find you home!"

"James! Oh, I'm so thankful to hear from
you!"

With all the understanding and tenderness of
his voice, Diana poured out all that was on her
heart to her brother. Always a good listener,
James let her tell him everything that had transpired.

"Sis, I'm sorry you've had to go through this.
I wish I were with you. I know what It's like—
remember Elizabeth?"

Diana thought of all that James had agonized
over when the girl he had been engaged to suddenly decided she did not love him enough for
marriage and had called the wedding off. His
pride, apart from his heart, had been deeply hurt.

"It takes time, Diana, but you'll see your
prayers answered. God does heal all our hurts
eventually. Anyway, it still may be that Chris is
the right one for you. Right now I'd like to punch
him on the nose, but perhaps it's all for the best.
You would be leaving America if you married him

and would have to get used to another culture. Even though we speak the same language, we're poles apart."

As they talked, Diana felt comforted. Remembering James's play, she changed the subject.

"James, I'm so delighted about the play! Forgive me for rambling on about my troubles. How are the rehearsals going?"

"They're wonderful. Sam Winton is a great director and the cast is superb. Do you think you can get to the first night? I'm counting on you being there."

"I'll be seeing El Crusto tomorrow morning and I'll ask him then." The thought of encountering her editor made Diana feel apprehensive, but she would try her very best to get to New York for the opening.

★   ★   ★

The offices of *Celebrity Homes* magazine were already charged with activity as Diana pushed her way through the entrance doors. Carrying her masses of notes from San Francisco and gifts from England for her fellow workers, she did not see her editor, Tom Bartlett, watching her from his office way down the corridor.

"Diana!" he roared. "In here!"

Knowing that the world was about to come to an end, she threw down the gifts on the reception desk, and with a nervous smile to the receptionist she walked quickly to her boss's office.

"Well, you're finally back," he said rather crossly. It was obvious that the morning was not going well with him and that he needed a second cup of coffee. His desk was piled high with correspondence, and the papers in the URGENT trays were cascading perilously over the metal sides. Tom Bartlett's already-craggy, creased face seemed to be even more so, and his thinning hair drooped over his forehead. Diana was conscious of him looking at her very intently through his horn-rimmed glasses.

Diana handed him the completed articles from England and he muttered, "Fine, fine. Finished the article on the Gary Mansion yet?"

"Mr. Bartlett—"

"Call me Tom," he said brusquely.

"Tom" (the name still did not come easily to her), "I only got back from San Francisco last night. I intend to work on it today."

"Fine, but we need it immediately. Where are the photographs?"

"Ian Kingsley will have them for you in a day or so."

"Not good enough—I need them today. Ethel!" he bellowed to his secretary next door, "Get Ian Kingsley on the phone. Tell him we need his works of art TODAY!"

"How am I ever going to ask him if I can go to New York next week for James's opening?" Diana agonized to herself.

"Diana, I hate to have to tell you this..."

"Here it comes..." She knew that something was afoot as soon as she had entered the office. "He's dissatisfied about something and this is the grand exit line."

"You've been away so much, but I really need you to cover a story back East. It's the Blanchard Penthouse in New York."

Trying to act calmly and not expressing any clue that she wanted to hug him, she said casually, "Oh, really? When do I need to go?"

"Real soon. Say the fifteenth? That will give you a week there—there's a lot to cover."

"There *certainly* will be," agreed Diana, relieved, excited, bewildered all at the same time. It would mean that she could be with James for his opening night, and her excitement just burst out as she thanked Tom Bartlett for letting her go.

His telephone rang and now he was caught up in some last-minute changes before the magazine went to press. As Diana left he called out to her, "I need the Gary article 'like yesterday,' Diana."

Diana turned and smiled at him. "But of course...*Tom!*"

Later, back in her office, she telephoned Ian with her news.

"Didn't I say you usually get what you want, somehow or other?" he said somewhat sardonically. From his tone Diana detected that he was in one of his moods, and she chose to ignore the sarcasm.

"You were right, Ian. It couldn't have happened at a better time, this Blanchard article. I can hardly believe it. James will be so thrilled."

With a promise to get together with Ian as soon as she finished the Gary Mansion article (and with a dig from him about her editor's impatience concerning his photographs—"Tell him I'm not some hack that churns out inferior work"), she got down to piecing together her notes into an excellent account of the old house's history and grand interior. As she typed she made a mental note to call Irene Shannon and find out how she was.

That evening Diana phoned James and told him the news. Together they laughed and talked like they had years before, when brother and sister had been so close. James would be in the throes of final rehearsals when she arrived in New York, but he would get to see her, even if only briefly before the play opened.

After talking to James, Diana called Ian and made plans to dine at his house the next evening. She would be leaving for New York the following morning, and he wanted to have a long talk.

Chapter Ten

Before dinner, just as the sun was beginning to set, Ian and Diana walked along the golden beach at Malibu. A neighbor's dog came up to them, and Ian threw a stick into the sea for him. As they watched, the dog would go to the brink of the water, then decide to retreat, turning to

look at them for help. Then with a sudden burst
of courage he would plow into the water and retrieve the stick. Tiring of the game, the dog ran
off to his owner, leaving Ian and Diana to continue their walk along the almost-deserted beach.

Little was said as Ian, with his arm around
Diana's shoulders, looked far off into the horizon.

"There's nothing like a California sunset, is
there?" Diana whispered, not wanting to break
the spell of the hypnotic beauty of the radiant light
that made the ocean seem as if it were being consumed by fire. Then, quite suddenly, the sun descended below the horizon and a darkness fell as
their part of the world prepared for night.

"It's not hard to believe there's a God when
you see a sunset."

Diana's statement brought Ian's thoughts back
to California. He had been remembering previous
beautiful sunsets, when their heralding of night
had brought a blessed relief from the sight of the
carnage around him. Flashes of the horrors he had
witnessed in Vietnam still haunted him, and they
were never predictable. A simple everyday happening like a sunset would trigger violent memories.

"God, Diana? We've been through all this
before. I'm sure He's there, but He is powerless.
He chooses to turn His face away from all the suffering." Ian suddenly broke away from her and

began to run toward his house. Diana watched him, feeling inadequate—unable to express her belief in a God that did care, that agonized over the suffering of the world.

When she walked up the steps leading to the deck surrounding Ian's house, she could hear him working in the kitchen, chopping food angrily. Diana leaned against the open door, watching him as he seemed to be taking out his frustrations on the innocent carrots and onions that would be part of their salad.

"Ian..."

"Let's not start a preaching series, Diana. I'm not in the mood for it." He threw lettuce, tomatoes, carrots, and onions into a large bowl and began to toss them vigorously with the herb dressing he had made.

"Fine, only go easy on the salad. It really hasn't done anything to you, Ian."

He looked angrily at her for a moment and then laughed. "Sorry, I do get dramatic, don't I? The lettuce is probably bruised beyond repair. The chef at L'Escoffier would have a fit." He wiped his hands on a towel and then came over to Diana.

"There's so much going on inside me right now. I don't know where I'm coming from. I'm still reeling from the news of your conquest in England, I guess."

Diana started to say something, but Ian continued, "Maybe, Diana, I should start dating too. I've put you on a pedestal and it's not fair to you. If you're not ready to marry me, let's both play the field and see how it goes from there."

She immediately began to feel insecure. Her feelings were still strong for Ian, and she hated the idea of him dating other women—she remembered Irene Shannon and the intense jealousy she had felt. Yet she *had* dated Chris. Chris...he seemed so far away, and more and more each day her time with him in England seemed almost unreal, as if he had been part of a movie and not a real-life encounter.

Diana lit the candles on the table in the dining alcove that overlooked the ocean while Ian whipped up a gourmet omelet.

They sat eating in silence. Each looked at the other, not knowing what to say.

"I wish you were coming to New York, Ian."

"It's impossible. I have a cover to do for *Vogue* tomorrow. Should be quite an interesting session. Jessica Bradley is sitting for it." He casually went on eating, sensing the raw nerve he had touched in Diana. Jessica had always openly flirted with Ian in front of Diana, whenever they had met in public. He got up from the table and went into his study, bringing back two large glossy photographs of her.

"What a face! She's a dynamite. Look at that

perfect bone structure! She doesn't have an angle that isn't fantastic.''

Diana reached for another roll, as if to say, "Who wants to be *that* thin anyway?'' She refrained from making any comment, but was seething inside. So *this* was what Ian's "I should start dating'' was all about! The roll felt like heavy cement inside her, but she continued talking about New York as if nothing bothered her.

As she cleared away the dishes, Ian went to the refrigerator and got out the dessert that Diana had brought—a strawberry flan. She thought she could easily be tempted to push it into his face. Instead, she said quietly, "I don't think I'll stay for dessert, Ian. It's getting late.''

"It's only 8:15—hardly late. Sit down and eat some of your delightful cooking.''

"You know I bought it at Gelson's!'' she shouted, his sarcastic tone making her overreact. She ran into the living room and picked up her handbag. Ian blocked her off as she was heading for the front door.

"Diana, stop behaving like an idiotic, jealous adolescent.''

"I'm not jealous. Why should I be?''

"Why is it all right for you to have another love and not me?'' Ian asked pointedly.

"I'm still confused by it all. I don't know how I feel.'' Breaking away, she rushed out the door.

"Well, Diana," he called after her, "when you do...let me know...if I'm still around." He looked at her long and hard as he stood framed by the opening of the front door.

Diana ran down the steps to her car. The evening traffic on the Pacific Coast Highway swept past her as she fumbled with her car key. Driving off, she did not even look back at Ian. She took the long route by the ocean back to her apartment in Brentwood.

Angry and bewildered, she thought of Jessica Bradley. Ian was going to be with her tomorrow. She began to imagine the scene as he whispered to Jessica while he photographed her, "Wonderful, darling. What a face! Smile...oh, *perfect,* darling!" The studio staff would bow and scrape to her and she would eat up all the attention. She *was* beautiful. Her face *was* perfect.

"God, why do I feel so jealous? If I don't really love Ian, why should I feel this way? Is it my pride? I hate myself for feeling this way."

Finally arriving at her apartment building, she parked her car in its stall in the underground garage and went up the elevator to her apartment. As she opened the front door, Diana heard the radio playing in the kitchen. Sarah was home. But Diana didn't feel like talking, especially to a model.

"Diana, darling! Welcome home. Sorry I was

away when you came home the other night. I had a wonderful session for the cover in Santa Barbara. The magazine is delighted with me and I feel so *thin*—I couldn't be happier." Sitting at the kitchen table, she was surrounded by avocados, honey, and ground nuts, and was giving herself a facial.

"Did I tell you I've found a new diet?"

"No, Sarah, you didn't, and quite frankly I don't have time to listen right now." Diana walked toward her bedroom.

"Ooh," said Sarah, "had a heavy day, huh? Me, too—I had a hair appointment and a manicure. Saw my agent, who says I *have* to get a new wardrobe, and so I had some fittings at Nieman's. So tiring standing there while they stick in all those pins. Honestly, Diana, I was worn out...Oh, by the way, did you meet any earls or dukes for me?"

Her voice droned on even after Diana shut her bedroom door. Deliberately she walked over to the closet, got out her suitcases, and started to pack. Hastily looking through her clothes, she saw the blue formal dress she had bought at Harrod's and decided to wear that to James's opening night. The memories that it triggered made Diana remember walking down the wide staircase at Drayton Castle with Chris by her side. It had been an exciting evening, one which had made her feel she had perhaps found the man she would marry.

Sweeping the dress into the suitcase along with a mass of tissue paper, she put those thoughts far from her mind.

The Blanchard Penthouse and James's play would fill her mind, and she looked forward to getting on that plane tomorrow and flying away from everything in Los Angeles.

Feeling rather guilty about her treatment of Sarah, she went back to the kitchen and talked to her over a cup of herbal tea. By this time the mask that Sarah had daubed her face with was thankfully beginning to tighten, making it almost impossible to understand her. Diana was in no mood to be asked about *any* of the aristocracy in England—or to hear about the hazards of a model's life.

The next morning the airport was crowded, with traffic backed up for blocks and tempers high. After the taxi dropped Diana off she managed to work her way through the crowd to the ticket counter for her seat assignment. Seeing that the plane was on time, she went through security and found a seat. She had brought a couple of rival magazines to peruse and quickly thumbed through one of them, anxious to read any articles on home interiors. As the magazine fell open to an advertisement for Cellini jewelry, Jessica Bradley's wide-eyed expression, with just a hint of a mocking smile, stared out at Diana, willing her to

become upset. Diana quickly shut the magazine.
   They announced that her flight was now ready
to board. She glanced at the clock—10 A.M. pre-
cisely. She knew that Ian was now beginning his
session with Jessica.
   What had Ian meant when he said, "...If I'm
still around"? Was he really getting interested in
Jessica? Diana sat in the plane, looking out at the
busy airport. They seemed so final, those words
of his as he stood in the doorway: "...If I'm still
around, Diana...."

Chapter Eleven

Diana looked out over Central Park from her room at the Park Tower Hotel. Located just down the street from The Plaza, this was the hotel she usually stayed at when in New York. She watched people as they walked together in the park and the horse-drawn carriages conveying couples for a romantic evening together. In the distance she could hear lions roaring in the zoo, making the scene seem almost unreal. The magic of being in New York was beginning to get to her. Her mind seemed to come alive here; even while walking down the streets it seemed that she was part of a great conspiracy, as if at any moment something wonderful would happen. Diana felt exhilarated at the prospect of being able to spend a week in this great, challenging city.

James would be meeting her at The Plaza after 10 P.M., and she couldn't wait to see him. Going over to the mirror in her room, she noted that there were dark circles under her eyes. She hastily camoflaged them, for she wanted her brother to see her at her best. Flipping her hair up at the ends, she looked at herself and decided that the plane ride, though tiring, had not been too destructive. Looking at her watch, she decided to start toward the Plaza even though she was still a little early. The hotel intrigued her, and she enjoyed looking at its classy gift shops.

As she entered the lobby, she attracted the attention of several men standing there. Diana ignored them and kept her eyes on the shop windows, absorbed by their elegant offerings. She was looking at one of the jewelry store's dazzling displays when she felt a hand on her shoulder. Startled, she turned in protest, then found herself

looking into her brother James's welcome hazel
eyes.

"James!"

"Hi, Sis!"

They embraced and kept hugging for quite a
while. The men who had been interested in the
tall, willowy blonde looked away, thinking that
she was more than occupied for the evening.

James looked tired; the strain of the rehearsals
really showed. But his face was as handsome as
ever. His clothes looked rather rumpled, but
Diana remembered that they always did. He never
seemed to have time for mere clothes. "When I'm
a star I'll have a valet and then you'll be
satisfied," he used to say to her when she would
tell him his suit needed pressing.

"Let's go have something to eat, Diana—I'm
starved."

They made their way to the Oak Room and
were ushered to a table in a secluded corner.

"This is perfect—I want to talk your head off,
James," Diana said contentedly. "You'll never
know how much I miss having you around."

"Move to New York and you can see me any-
time you want to."

With all that had been happening between her
and Ian, Diana wondered if that might not be a
good idea. While she was here, perhaps she would
make some inquiries about a position with one

of the New York-based magazines. As they talked the hours slipped by, and had it not been that the waiter's expression was becoming a little less delighted to see them, they would not have realized that it was after midnight. Drinking the last of her coffee, Diana told James they must be going.

"Yes, we're doing a complete run-through of the play tomorrow. Then the next day it's dress rehearsal. Temperaments are riding high and everyone is walking on eggshells. We're all wondering how the critics will be. Because it's a revival, they have the last run of the play to compare us with in their minds. Let's hope they're kind."

"They'd better be—especially to my brother," said Diana defensively. "I'm so thrilled to be here for the opening night, James. If Tom Bartlett hadn't let me come I would have died a little inside."

"So would I. Knowing that you'll be in the front is going to mean so much to me, Diana." He suddenly remembered something. "You're invited to the party afterward at Sardi's—which reminds me. Who's going to escort you to the play?"

"I hadn't even thought about that!" laughed Diana. "I'll feel foolish arriving alone but all dressed up. Maybe one of the men on the Blanchard Penthouse assignment would like to accompany me. I'll let you know tomorrow."

James walked her to the Park Tower Hotel and then went back to his studio apartment off Third Avenue. Diana watched him walk away, thankful for a brother she could really talk to. But as she walked to the elevator she realized that he was the one who had done most of the talking. At this moment his mind was so full of the play and Sir Thomas More and his fight of conscience with Henry the Eighth. She would wait until after the opening to have a heart-to-heart talk with him.

She was about to enter the elevator when she wondered if there might be any message for her at the reception desk. A pink piece of paper lay there. The clerk handed it to her with a "Have a good night, Miss Lewis," and she proceeded once more to the elevator, reading:

> Diana,
> Cover a Cavanaugh Advertising Agency's
> press conference at the Waldorf tomorrow
> at 11 A.M.
>
>   Tom Bartlett

"Great," thought Diana. "Any excuse to go to the Waldorf!"

The next morning Diana decided to walk to the Blanchard Penthouse on Park Avenue. The air was humid and the prediction was for thunderstorms in the late afternoon; the temperature

would soar to the upper nineties. She had dressed
in a light, flimsy Laura Ashley dress. The small
floral design and the texture of the material made
her look cool and assured as she walked down
59th Street and crossed over Fifth Avenue with
its luringly tempting department stores. She passed
the bustling, competitive world of advertising that
was Madison Avenue and came to the stately, dignified atmosphere of Park Avenue. Turning left,
she proceeded up the avenue to the building where
Estelle Blanchard had her penthouse. The doorman gave a questioning but appreciative look as
she approached him. Then, assured of her creden-
tials, he allowed her through the imposing lobby
to the elevator, having telephoned her arrival to
the Blanchard butler.

Diana stepped out into an entrance hall that
almost defied description; yet she knew that this
is what her writing would have to accomplish. The
building was sumptuous; its marble floors seemed
to take up an entire city block.

Diana was ushered up the spiral staircase
leading to the second floor of the penthouse and
then in to meet the wealthy but widowed million-
airess Estelle Blanchard. In her sixties, she remained an elegant and exceptionally well-groomed
woman. She was attired in pale-gold satin pa-
jamas. The Southern accent surprised Diana as
Mrs. Blanchard welcomed her to the "little escape

from the horrors of Manhattan. I just get so homesick for my estate outside of Atlanta, honey." Leading Diana to a chair which overlooked the brilliant skyline, Mrs. Blanchard gracefully arranged herself on a long, lean chaise lounge and went on. "It's part of the price you pay when you are encumbered with wealth and financial responsibilities."

"This is simply breathtaking, Mrs. Blanchard. Perhaps you would tell me a little about the refurbishing of the apartment and what made you decide on such a modern decor?"

Estelle Blanchard proceeded to say that being surrounded by ultramodern furnishings would be a constant reminder that this was only a place to stay and to entertain in occasionally, but that it was not her *home*. "That is in Atlanta, honey, and I just can't wait to get back there. But business calls, and this is a most convenient little 'pied-a-terre' for me."

The "little pied-a-terre," Diana discovered, had eight bedrooms, all with private bathrooms, endless hallways, two large reception rooms, a library, a dining room, a breakfast nook, servants' quarters, and a terrace that rivaled the gardens of Europe. Vines, azaleas, and rhododendrons grew in profusion. Terra-cotta urns, filled with masses of geraniums, framed a secluded corner where a table set for two awaited Mrs. Blanchard and a guest for lunch. They would dine overlooking the insistently dramatic skyline of Manhattan.

"It's such a responsibility, all this," sighed Mrs. Blanchard, waving her perfectly manicured hands in a desperate gesture. "I just wish my Alfred were still alive to take care of all the infuriating legal and financial details. Honestly, honey, my mind spins sometimes with it all. Give me the days when all I had to do was enjoy his pampering me and sending me off on a shopping expedition. It's enough to drive my *crazy.*"

Diana was beginning to feel stifled by this obviously spoiled and empty woman's conversation. Being an outspoken person many times herself, she now found it hard not to tell this pampered woman just how fortunate she was. Diana kept looking at her watch, willing the hands to move faster so she could excuse herself and escape the claustrophobic world of her hostess. Mrs. Blanchard was becoming bored with the interview too.

"Honey, I'm expecting a guest for lunch, so perhaps you wouldn't mind..."

Jumping up, Diana told her she really had another appointment too, and had to leave. With a promise that the decorator and his staff would be here in the afternoon, Mrs. Blanchard went through the motions of graciously escorting Diana to the elevator.

Diana had never been so glad to see an elevator

door open. In a flash she entered her way of escape, and with a promise that she would be back in the afternoon the doors closed on the world of Mrs. Blanchard and all her "responsibilities."

The humid air that greeted her as she emerged through the revolving doors out to Park Avenue felt almost refreshing to Diana. She was free, if only for a few hours, from the cloying, whining personality of Estelle Blanchard.

Diana hailed a taxi and asked to be taken to the Waldorf. Powdering her nose and replacing her lipstick, she felt relaxed. She did not have a clue as to what the Cavanaugh Advertising Agency's press conference was about, but she looked out the taxi window and enjoyed watching the New Yorkers' expressions as they rushed to their seemingly life-and-death appointments.

The taxi pulled up to the grand entrance of the Waldorf Astoria. Well-dressed men and women were filing in, together with what seemed to be a horde of reporters and photographers. Diana paid the taxi driver and joined their ranks. As she walked up the wide, opulent staircase she noticed the brilliant crystal chandeliers and the luxurious decor for which the Waldorf was renowned throughout the world.

The dignified notice board in the lobby informed Diana where the Cavanaugh press conference was being held. A crowd of photographers and reporters was heading down a long corridor, and Diana followed automatically. Inside the room a long table and a microphone had been set up, and lights were being adjusted. Diana found a seat not too far back and got her notebook and pencil out of her handbag. She had hoped that someone she knew from the West Coast would be representing her hometown newspaper, but as she looked at the assortment of faces, no one seemed familiar to her. Someone from the agency began distributing brochures when a side door opened and in walked two obviously Madison Avenue types. They were followed by a tall, handsome, blond young man—dressed in a Savile Row suit—followed by a very attractive young woman with dark, immaculately groomed hair.

Diana sat transfixed. It was Chris! Chris and his sister Margaret! "What in the world are they doing here. Why didn't I know that he would be in New York?"

Chapter Twelve

It took Diana a full five minutes before she could even begin to pull herself together. The advertising man had been explaining the reason for the press conference, but she had not heard a word of it. Chris had not yet seen Diana and she was grateful for the rather large gentleman sitting in front of her.

Diana heard Drayton Castle mentioned, and gradually she became aware of what the conference was all about. The castle was being opened to the public, and this event had coincided with British Week in New York. The Earl of Drayton had decided to send his son and daughter to the United States to represent the family and to drum up business for their ancestral home.

Apart from the daily visitors that would be coming to the castle, the Draytons were opening a wing for guests to stay overnight. A weekend package had been worked out, and those staying at the castle would mingle with the family, dining with them and being entertained in a grand way. Diana thought of how all this must be affecting Lady Drayton, who had resisted any change. "Imagine Estelle Blanchard arriving on their doorstep and having to be entertained for a weekend! It would be too much, even for the sake of saving the castle," she thought.

Chris was introduced as being the heir to this "historically magnificent castle." He stood up rather hesitantly and then proceeded to tell the press of the merits and splendor of his home. A projector showed slides of the castle as Chris spoke.

The large gentleman seated in front of Diana

leaned forward suddenly to retrieve some papers he had dropped, and it was then that Chris saw Diana sitting there. Their eyes met, and it seemed as if there were no one else in the room. Chris faltered for a few moments, but with a quick kick from his sister, the Lady Margaret, he continued his short talk.

Questions were asked for what seemed ages to Diana, and then there was another lengthy explanation by the advertising company's representative. Cameras flashed, and after a few brief words of thanks, the conference came to an end. Reporters surrounded Chris and Margaret, asking for interviews. All the time Chris had been very conscious of Diana sitting there, looking absolutely gorgeous. When Chris could finally break away, he came over to her. Somewhat embarrassed, he said, "Hello, Diana, aren't you going to welcome me to your incredible country?"

Diana still felt stunned and at a loss for words. She looked at this handsome young man that only a week or so before she had thought she was in love with. She could only answer with, "Well... welcome, Chris. I can only say that it's an enormous surprise to see you here."

The Lady Margaret had been watching her brother intently, and as the conversation with the exquisite blonde continued, it really began to annoy her. They had not come over to New York to satisfy her brother's constant search for female conquests. Margaret was conscious too that this reporter was monopolizing Chris when there were so many others who wanted to speak to him. Walking over to his side, she pointedly told him that others were waiting to talk with him.

Chris turned to his sister and said, "Margaret, this is Diana Lewis, who stayed with us while you were in Europe."

Diana looked at Margaret and saw her expression of surprise and concern. "So this is the famous Diana we have heard so much about. How do you do?" Her voice sounded like an iceberg encountering the Titanic.

Diana's first impression of Margaret from her photograph on the piano in the living room at Drayton Castle had been right. She was cool and assured, and obviously nothing would stop her from obtaining what she wanted. The perfectly tailored summer suit made the Lady Margaret an imposing, striking young woman—beautiful in a harsh, dramatic kind of way.

"I enjoyed my vacation at the castle so much," Diana heard herself say.

"So I hear," the Lady Margaret answered in a slightly sarcastic voice. Chris, sensing that Diana was feeling extremely uncomfortable, interjected, "Why don't we have a spot of lunch? I'm absolutely starved. There was so much to do before the conference that I hardly had time for even a cup of tea this morning.''

"Michael Cavanaugh has invited us to lunch, Chris,'' Margaret said pointedly. By this time she was finding it almost impossible to keep her temper.

"Then why don't you join him, and I'll see you back at the suite later on.''

Chris took hold of Diana's elbow and escorted her out of the room, leaving a thoroughly frustrated and indignant Margaret to explain the absence of her brother.

Diana and Chris found a table for two in the hotel's restaurant, near Peacock Alley, and as they listened to a pianist playing soft, intimate music, their moods of bewilderment and uncertainty began to disappear. It seemed as if they had not experienced any parting—that this could have been a restaurant in London. Studying the menu, Diana found herself remembering the drive to the airport, when Chris had pulled the car over to the side of the road and kissed her, telling her how much he would miss her...then the telephone conversation...

Chris's voice interrupted her thoughts. "Diana, will you forgive me for being such an idiot on the phone the other day? I've tried to get you several times, but you had either checked out of the hotel or you weren't in your apartment.''

"You sounded so distant, as if you didn't care if we ever met again." Diana looked at him questioningly.

"I know. I was so stunned by hearing Ian's voice that I immediately thought the worst. I was judging you, I suppose, in the light of *my* past." He leaned forward and took her hands, wanting desperately to take her in his arms. Then he looked at her wrists. "You're not wearing my bracelet," he said sadly.

"Do you blame me, Chris?"

"Diana, I really do love you. Please forget the phone conversation and let's start over again, as if nothing happened. The main reason I pushed this trip was to get over here and try to see you. You can't imagine all that has been going on during these last few days. I'm still completely confused by it all. When you left, my father and I began seriously planning for the opening of the castle. He had studied his financial situation and realized that we had to act fast or else it would mean selling the castle and having to begin again somewhere else. It would have killed my mother— you know how attached she is to it all."

Diana nodded. She had a deep affection for Lady Drayton, a person who genuinely seemed to love people and was concerned for their welfare—the exact opposite of Estelle Blanchard. Diana told Chris about the woman she had been interviewing before coming over to the Waldorf.

Changing the subject, Chris took Diana's hand again. "Diana, I remember so vividly the last night you were at the castle and I knocked on your bedroom door to take you down to dinner. I'll never forget how you looked—the beautiful blue dress shimmering in the candlelight and your eyes seeming to shine even brighter. I believe you were very sure of what your answer would be even before I asked you."

Diana laughed rather nervously. "Maybe I thought so, but marriage is a very important step. I was and still am concerned about the difference in our backgrounds. It's not a decision I can come to impulsively. It's forever as far as I'm concerned."

"Me too," and he reached out to touch her cheek.

After the waiter had taken their order, Diana, changing the subject, told him about James opening in a play the next night. "I'm so thrilled for him. Will you be here tomorrow?" Chris nodded. "Would you like to accompany me?"

"I'd love to, Diana."

"I'm not sure if I can get a ticket for your sister."

"Don't worry about her. Knowing Margaret, she probably already has something lined up. We Draytons live dangerously." As soon as he had said that, he wished he could take back the words. A cloud seemed to cross Diana's eyes. "I know," she said.

Was Chris still thinking of her as one of his latest acquisitions or did he really love her?

As if he read her thoughts, he whispered, "But not since I met you. You'll never know how lonely I felt after you left...I've never experienced anything like it. I don't want to waste my life anymore, Diana. I want to spend all my days with you." Looking at her very directly, he said, "My nights, too."

The waiter arrived with their salads, and Diana was thankful for the interruption. When she was with Chris her whole being seemed to be invaded by his magnetic personality.

"Diana..." Chris's voice brought her back to him. "Are you free for dinner tonight?" She shook her head apologetically. "No, I have to go back to the penthouse this afternoon and I don't know when I'll finish."

"Well, how about a late dinner somewhere? Why don't you call me when you're through? I'll be working in our suite."

After coffee Diana realized the time and told Chris she had to make her way back to Mrs. Blanchard's. Chris said quickly, "First come up to the suite. I want to show you the great 'blowups' we have of the castle that the agency is going to put in the travel agents' windows." He saw her hesitation. "Now that does sound like a line, but my dear sister is bound to be back by now."

Diana agreed to go with him, and in the elevator, in front of several rather dignified elderly people, Chris kissed her on her nose. Then, as the elevator ascended he kissed her on the lips—slowly and deliberately. Embarrassed, Diana stepped back into the arms of a bemused gentleman, who obviously enjoyed the encounter.

Margaret was busy talking to some people when Chris and Diana entered the suite. The welcome mat was obviously not out for Diana, and she sensed Margaret's displeasure even more. Chris seemed to ignore his sister and began showing Diana the splendid posters of the castle. Looking at them, Diana saw the lake they sat by that last night, the chapel, and her bedroom windows in the west tower. She felt almost homesick.

"They're really beautiful, Chris. How could anyone resist staying there?" She asked him for more of the literature. "I know our editor will want to do a big article on the castle."

"Perhaps he'll send you over soon," Chris said hopefully.

"I think I could write it all from memory, Chris," and she turned away from him, feeling rather emotional. She stood looking out the window, watching the traffic stream down Park

Avenue. From the 25th floor the taxis looked like long yellow ribbons as they drove bumper to bumper.

"I've been wondering what that church is down there. Its architecture is so unusual. The vast dome looks like an enormous mosaic," Chris said, with his hand on Diana's shoulder.

"That's St. Bartholomew's Episcopal Church. I've always been intrigued by it too. It's built in the Byzantine style." Diana remembered, "They have wonderful lunchtime concerts. If you're free, perhaps we could go tomorrow?"

"Well, I'm not sure what's on the schedule, but I'll let you know." Chris was feeling the heat from his sister as she stood listening to their conversation.

Diana glanced at her watch and realized that she should have been back at the penthouse 15 minutes earlier. Making a very fast exit, she promised to call Chris when she was through later that evening.

As Diana sat in the taxi going up Park Avenue, thunderclouds were beginning to roll into Manhattan. The eerie, oppressive atmosphere that precedes such a storm made her even more aware of the conflict that was going on inside her. She wondered if the irresistible charm of Chris would make her want to forget all that she had ever believed in...

Chapter Thirteen

The thunderstorm was nothing short of spectacular as viewed from the windows of the Blanchard Penthouse. Lightning pierced the blackened sky and it seemed to Diana as if she were watching a divine fireworks display. Rain beat against the windows, making the skyline of Manhattan appear like a blurred, impressionistic watercolor.

The photographer and the designer were still discussing suitable angles and shots. It had been a long evening, with only one dramatic entrance by Estelle Blanchard as she left for "a most important dinner engagement. My time is just not my own," she had sighed, leaving her delighted staff and Diana to fend for themselves.

As Diana wandered through the penthouse, she wondered if wealth were really worth all the effort that seemed to go with being able to hold onto it. Even those who enjoyed being wealthy seemed to be driven constantly, fearing loss of the prestige and position that meant so much to them. The Drayton family appeared to be different, even though they too were struggling to survive. The exception was the Lady Margaret. She was tenacious in her drive for promoting the family and her position in society. If Diana were to marry Chris, she wondered if Margaret would ever accept her, or whether it would always be a tense, unrelenting relationship with her sister-in-law.

Diana glanced at her watch. It was almost 10:30 P.M. She called the Waldorf and got through to Chris's suite.

"Hello?"

"Chris, it's your blonde American friend and she's dying of hunger."

"Diana! Same here. Where are you?"

"Still at the penthouse, but I've decided I have enough material for my article."

"Wonderful! Tell me the address and I'll pick you up immediately."

Diana told him where she was and hung up the telephone. Excitedly she gathered her things together and called out "good night" to everyone. In the elevator she kept telling herself, "Don't let this get out of hand. If he asks you to marry him again tonight, wait until morning before you give your answer." But in her heart she knew what the answer would be, in spite of all the doubts that still seemed to surge within her. But Manhattan was an excitingly romantic setting, and she had to see everything in its right perspective.

Standing in the lobby, waiting for Chris, Diana watched the traffic make its swishing, watery way up and down Park Avenue. A taxi pulled up, letting Chris out in the pouring rain. Pushing her way around the revolving door, she found herself in his arms and he was kissing her. They laughingly jumped into the taxi and Chris asked the driver to take them to Le Jardin, a restaurant off Third Avenue. "It's a quiet little French restaurant that has been highly recommended to me." Diana didn't care where they ate—anywhere would have been fantastic to her at this moment.

They sat close together in the taxi, Chris whispering how lovely she was, "even though you look like a drowned rat!" He kissed her again as the driver watched through the rearview mirror.

After Chris paid the taxi driver, he and Diana ran down the winding steps leading to the basement restaurant and were ushered to a table way in the back of the candlelit room. It was delightfully decorated in white lattice and ferns, with charming French music playing softly in the background.

"I love this place," said Diana as she looked admiringly around the restaurant. "It's really charming. Whoever recommended it should be thanked profusely."

Chris was not even listening to her—just looking at this vivacious young woman with an expression of delight. "Did I ever tell you that you are the most beautiful girl I've ever known?"

"Probably," Diana teased as they held hands across the table. "But then you're not so bad-looking yourself."

Diana was experiencing a feeling of freedom as she sat with Chris, as if she could suddenly be herself with this man whom she had known for only a few weeks, even though it seemed forever.

Over dinner she told him more about the penthouse and the incredible view of the storm. He watched her intently as she talked animatedly. The soft light from the flickering candle made her look even more lovely.

"Chris, what was I talking about? I don't think you even heard a word."

"But of course...something about the rain, wasn't it?" He laughed and touched her face, tracing the incredible bone structure. "You'll love living in England—it rains all the time there."

Laughing, Diana looked at him questioningly. "And *who* says I'm going to live in England?"

"I do, and you know you are."

Diana wanted to say yes, but she knew she had to talk to Chris seriously about many things first. "Chris, we always seem to skirt the subject of Ian. Could we talk about him...*please?*"

"Diana, what is there to talk about? I know you really love me. If I were Ian I wouldn't want anyone who loved someone else. What kind of future would there be—always wondering if you were thinking of another love?"

His words "another love" triggered Diana's thoughts back to the last night she had seen Ian: "Why is it all right for you to have another love and not me?" Then as he stood in the doorway watching her leave: "Let me know...if I'm still around." The words seemed so final, and the 3000-mile distance between them now made it seem even more final.

"Now, you're not listening to *me.*"

"Oh, sorry. I was miles away."

"I know you were, and your thoughts were not about me, were they?"

"No, Chris. They weren't. I was remembering the last time I saw Ian. We had quite a serious argument. He made me extremely angry and I know why he did it. He was very hurt, *very* hurt about my feelings for you."

They sat for a few minutes without speaking, their hands intertwined and the music seeming to draw them closer together.

Diana broke the silence. "Have you talked to your family about us?"

"Yes, and they were delighted to think that they might have you for a daughter-in-law. You know my parents really enjoyed your stay. Believe me, the castle seemed even more enormous after you left. You lit up all the dark corners and brought a joy that had been missing for a long time."

"But what about your sister? I sense that she is, to say the least, disapproving of me."

Chris laughed. "Forget Margaret. She has always been that way. If anything happens that she has not been the instigator of, she gets put out for a while. In a short time she'll be saying it was all her idea." Chris laughed. "Actually, the reason why she's pouting is because she has been trying to pawn off her best friend on me. Delightful girl, if you like them podgy and dull."

"Well, there's something else that bothers me—your wealth."

"You mean our lack of it, don't you? You know I'm over here to try to save the family home."

"I know that, but even if you had to give up the castle, you would still be far wealthier than I have ever been."

Chris pushed his chair back and looked at her, his head to one side. "Do you want me to renounce my title? Turn my back on my inheritance and live on a desert island with you?"

"Of course not, Chris," Diana said amusedly.

"I'd be willing to, if that's what you want," he said very seriously.

"No, it isn't, Chris. I'm not questioning you. I'm questioning myself. I want to know that I love you for *you*—not the castle or your title."

"That's very noble of you, Diana. I don't have any fears along that line. When I'm with you something wonderful happens. I find myself believing in our future together. It's as if I'm complete at last."

Diana looked at him, knowing that this was exactly how she felt too. Yet she still could not commit herself...there were still too many questions to resolve...

Chris said quietly, "Diana, you mentioned that you would like to go to a lunchtime concert at

St. Bartholomew's—could we go tomorrow?''

She thought of all there was still to do regarding her article and how she had planned to stay at her hotel to finish typing it before going to James's opening night.

"I can't tomorrow, Chris. Could we make it the day after?''

He nodded. "Good. I'll plan on it *and* on taking you to the theater tomorrow night. James must be exhausted—wasn't the dress rehearsal today?''

"Yes. He looks very tired, but he's so thrilled to be in this play that he would rehearse 24 hours a day if necessary. By the way, we're invited to the first-night party at Sardi's afterward, so you'll be seeing the way Broadway celebrates.''

He picked up the candle from the center of the table and leaned over to kiss her.

Regretfully they realized that the time was getting late, so they left to walk up the winding staircase to the pavement outside. Protectively, he walked beside her with his arm around her.

The rain had stopped and the skies had cleared. For a brief few hours the air in New York smelled fresh and exhilarating. Diana felt as if her whole life was just beginning. All the loneliness and all the doubts were being swept away with the cool breeze that brushed her face and hair.

Chapter Fourteen

The entrance to the Morosco Theater, on West 45th Street, was jammed with autograph hunters and the first-night audience valiantly trying to battle their way through them.

As Diana and Chris stepped out of their taxi, one of the crowd shouted, "She's got to be *some-*

body!'' Another shouted, "So has he!" The crowd lunged at them with their autograph books and pencils. Chris looked at Diana and grinned, "I should jolly well hope so!" as he escorted her through the pushing, wild-eyed mob.

After they finally managed to get to their seats, Chris said amusedly, "I do believe our first-night crowds in London are a little less demanding than yours. But then ours would probably be just as wild if they saw you, especially in that exquisite dress." Diana was wearing the romantic blue dress she had bought at Harrod's. He gazed at her admiringly. "I'm glad you wore it tonight, Diana."

She smiled at him, looking absolutely radiant. The diaphanous material sparkled even as the houselights dimmed. The audience hushed as the curtain went up, and Diana said a prayer in her heart for her brother. Earlier that day she had sent him a telegram wishing him personal success. As she watched she felt such pride; she was so happy to be there on his special night. Seated next to Chris, with his hand in hers, she found it difficult to concentrate on the play completely.

When the final curtain came down, it was obvious that this revival of "A Man for All Seasons" had been a triumph. The comments from everyone around them were all superlatives. Later, backstage, Diana hugged James, praising him for his performance. She introduced him to Chris, and there was that "big brother look" that came into James's eyes as he tried to decide if Lord Christopher Drayton were worthy of his sister. Above all, James did not want to see her get hurt. He remembered how upset she had been on the telephone that night after Chris had seemed so distant to her. Chris sensed James's hesitancy to accept him completely. The coldness shown by James made Chris think, "My sister Margaret and James should get together. Them seem to have a lot in common!"

As they all walked into Sardi's Restaurant on West 44th Street, James was applauded by the guests already there—in the tradition that had started years before on first nights. Mr. Sardi himself congratulated him and then graciously welcomed them all to his famed and unique restaurant. The sight of all the caricatures of famous actors and actresses that decorated the walls made Diana remark to James, "Keep this up and your face will be there soon!" James laughed, beginning to relax. "Who knows!" he said hopefully.

When they were seated, Diana looked around at the guests gathered there—so many faces, beautiful starlets, and celebrities from New York's society. She watched Chris's face. If he would be tempted in any way to be lured by one of these beautiful women, there seemed to be no sign. His attention was completely on her, as if none of them really existed. Christopher Drayton had tired of his search for conquest. He had found Diana, and now there was no one else who could possibly interest him.

They decided to leave James at the party and walk back to Diana's hotel. It was apparent that James was beginning to warm up to Chris. "Now to convince my sister would be the last hurdle," Chris thought, convinced that Diana would say yes.

For a few blocks Diana and Chris walked hand in hand, happy to be with each other, and deep in thought. Diana was remembering the play. The daughter of Sir Thomas More had mentioned being anchored to principles. She thought how her whole life seemed to have been based on principles. But were they enough? When faced with a challenge to them, so often she had wanted to give in. Now as she walked with Chris, she thought of how she longed to be with him and how easy it would be for her to say yes if he asked to come up to her hotel room. No one would know.

When they arrived at her hotel, Chris said he would walk to the elevator with her. They stood for a moment looking into each other's eyes—a million words unsaid. Then when the elevator doors opened, Chris said, "Good night, my lovely Diana. We have a date at St. Bartholomew's tomorrow at noon. See you then." He kissed her and left, leaving her somewhat amazed and thankful. At that moment it would have been difficult for her to say no, and he had sensed it.

Walking back to the Waldorf, Chris was thinking of many questions the play had raised. Would he have had the conviction to go to his death for a principle, like Sir Thomas More—who had been beheaded because he was a man who valued his conscience more than his life? Chris especially remembered the third act, where Sir Thomas More had stated that his sacrifice was simply a matter of love—love for the God who had become so real to him.

These were heady thoughts for Chris, who until recently had merely wanted to live for a good time. Now he had met Diana and had seen what was so important in her life. He remembered their last night in England together by the lake when she had shared her beliefs. Her sincerity had touched something in him that had lain dormant for years—a need to know more of the God who was so important to Diana.

★　　★　　★

St. Bartholomew's was crowded when Diana arrived. She looked for Chris but could not find him, so decided to sit in a pew near the back to watch for him. The worshipfulness of this great church was welcoming to her. She had not slept well—her thoughts had been so much on Chris and the questions the play had raised. Diana now knew that she really loved him, but could she marry someone if he did not believe as she did? She was back to the same questions that had tormented her about Ian.

As the orchestra assembled, she felt Chris's hand on her shoulder. He sat beside her and kissed her briefly, whispering, "Lots to tell you." Diana smiled at him as together they listened to the glorious Mass in C Minor by Mozart. Diana and Chris were both caught up in the worship and magnificence of it all. Looking at him, she saw that he was deeply moved.

The concert over, they remained seated as people filed past them. When the church was empty, Chris turned to Diana and said quietly, "Thank you for leading me back."

"Leading you back?" she whispered.

Chris nodded. "Yes. Since I met you I've felt a need to know God's love and forgiveness...and you have brought me back."

Diana looked at him, tears forming in her eyes.

"Chris, I've been looking at my own life, and last night the play made me realize that merely *living* the principles of Jesus Christ is not enough...I need to *love* Him more." She told Chris of the day she had visited the church in London where her parents' memorial service had been.

"I read the words of a hymn we had sung so many times, yet I never really understood them: 'The King of Love My Shepherd Is.' The line that stood out to me was, 'I nothing lack if I am His and He is mine forever.' Just today I've realized that I've only been going through the motions of being a Christian. Oh, I've tried to be moral and good, but still I've never really known what it means to be His, and I want to, Chris."

"So do I," he whispered. "I've been thinking about it all night."

Diana looked at the gold cross gleaming on the altar. "Jesus must have loved us so much...He was willing to experience such suffering so that we might be forgiven."

Diana turned to him, her eyes bright with tears. "Why don't we give Him our lives right now, Chris?" She knelt and bowed her head, and a few seconds later Chris knelt beside her.

They prayed silently in the quietness of that great church, aware that their lives would never be the same again—that the Source of true love had entered their hearts and that He would guide them from now on.

Coming out into the sunshine, they walked down the church steps leading to Park Avenue, smiling at each other in a new and even more tender way.

Chapter Fifteen

꧁꧂

Chris and Diana stood at the corner of 51st Street and Park Avenue, waiting for the traffic light to change. They had not spoken since leaving the church, but had walked arm in arm, feeling closer than ever.

The light changed and they crossed the street,

making their way to the Waldorf. Halfway up the great staircase leading to the lobby, Chris stopped and said, "For the last time—Diana Lewis, will you marry me?"

Diana, her face glowing, shouted, "Oh, yes... yes!" They flung their arms around each other, unaware that people were having to push around them to ascend and descend the staircase. Diana dropped her handbag and an elderly gentleman retrieved it for her—delighted to be of service to such a radiant young woman.

"We had better move," Diana said to Chris. "We don't want to be the cause of an enormous pileup at the Waldorf." Laughing, they walked to the elegant lobby and sat down on one of the velvet benches, trying to comprehend all that had taken place in such a short time. People looked over at them as they sat there holding hands, their expressions telling the world of their happiness.

Chris suddenly remembered that he had to make a phone call, and with a promise of "Be back in a minute," he left Diana, who by now was shivering with joy. She wandered over to the gift shop and began to look at some souvenirs of New York, not really conscious of what she was seeing because her mind was racing with all that had happened. She was going to be married! She wanted to tell everyone!

The New York newspapers caught her eye. She

had read them at her hotel earlier that morning: The notices for James's play had been raves, and James himself had received excellent reviews. Diana noticed that the gift shop carried out-of-town newspapers, with the *Los Angeles Times* among them. It had been quite a few days since she had heard any news of home, so she bought a copy and carried it back to the lobby. She sat reading it, hardly concentrating as she kept looking up for any sign of Chris returning. Los Angeles was having Santa Ana winds, causing great concern during this fire season.

Turning the page, she continued reading. Then, in the upper right-hand corner of the third page she saw the headline:

FAMOUS PHOTOGRAPHER FIGHTING FOR LIFE AFTER HEAD-ON CRASH

Unbelievingly, she read on:

Ian Kingsley, renowned photographer, was critically injured in a head-on collision on Pacific Coast Highway in Malibu at 1:15 A.M. Thursday. His car was hit by a vehicle traveling in the opposite direction which crossed the dividing line. The driver of that car was killed instantly. Kingsley remains in intensive care at St. John's Hospital, Santa Monica, with massive injuries.

Kingsley first captured the attention of the American public when his photography...

Diana sat in shock, her hand over her mouth, trying to stifle an agonized cry. As Chris walked back to her, he saw the look of intense pain on her face. Diana stood and silently handed him the newspaper, unable to speak. He read the account of the accident and then said tenderly, "Diana, what can I say?"

"Just...hold me," she managed to whisper, "just hold me."

★   ★   ★

The flight back to Los Angeles was one of the longest Diana had ever known. She was thankful that Chris had insisted on coming with her, for the pain of Ian's accident would have been so hard for her to bear alone. Now Chris sat quietly beside her, and his presence gave her strength.

Looking out the window, she kept remembering Ian's last words to her: "...If I'm still around..." They haunted Diana. Were they prophetic? If they hadn't had that argument, would he have been on that highway? But it was ridiculous, she kept rationalizing to herself, because she would have been in New York anyway. But the guilt remained with her, and when she mentioned it to Chris he assured her, over and over again, that the accident had nothing to do with her.

"Diana," he said, quietly but determinedly, "we have to trust God for Ian's recovery." But she thought of their happiness and then of Ian lying mangled in an intensive care unit, fighting for his life. All the joy had been taken away from her—she didn't deserve happiness at this moment.

Dazed, she watched the plane land in Los Angeles. They walked down the aisle, through the long corridors or the airport, down to the baggage area, and into a taxi that would take them to Santa Monica. How she dreaded seeing Ian... dreaded seeing his handsome face possibly scarred...dreaded hearing the doctor's prognosis.

As they arrived at St. John's Hospital, Chris knew that it was not a time for words—just for the assurance of his being there with Diana.

They walked through the entrance, and Chris left Diana for a moment as he went over to the information desk to find out where Ian was. Diana looked around at the stark hospital surroundings and thought she must be dreaming all this—one of those hideous nightmares in which you wake up in the middle of the night and then find that it's just a dream. But Diana knew, unfortunately, that this was reality.

Chris came back and they walked to the elevator. It was empty when they got in, for which Diana was thankful—she could not bear to have people looking at her right now. She felt as if all her emotions were naked before everyone and that tears were only a fragile second away. Chris whispered, "Trust Him, Diana." She nodded. As the elevator door opened they walked toward the intensive care unit.

The nurses' station was vacant due to several emergencies that night. Chris asked Diana to sit down while they waited. As she did, she saw a solitary, dejected figure of a woman sitting in a far corner. Her long raven hair partly hid her face as she rocked to and fro in a despairing, pleading position. Diana recognized her—it was Jessica Bradley, the model whose name had touched off Diana's final argument with Ian. Looking at her, Diana saw the vulnerability and sorrow that etched her face. The sophistication was gone. Jessica was like everyone else when heartache bursts in unannounced into a person's life.

Diana went over to her and said hesitantly, "Jessica?" She looked up in astonishment. Reaching out to Diana, she held her hands.

"He's only just hanging on, Diana." Her eyes filled with tears. "I love him so...he's just *got* to live." The words poured out of her in desperation. "I'd just moved in with him...we were so happy...."

Diana sat down, dazed by her words: "I'd just moved in." Were they living together? It had only been a week since Diana had left for New York. Anger, sorrow, hurt, pride—all these emotions were charging through her. The hurt was there, and it mingled with the sorrow of Ian's fight for life.

A nurse returned to the station, and Diana walked over to her.

"Is it possible to see Ian Kingsley?" she asked in a hollow voice.

The nurse looked up and said briskly, "No visitors for Mr. Kingsley."

"But I've flown all the way from New York to see him?"

"Are you family?"

Diana shook her head. "No, but we were going to get married...once..." Diana didn't know what else to say.

The nurse looked at her now with full attention. "What is your name?"

"Diana Lewis."

"Oh...he's been asking for you. Just a minute, I'll see if you can go in."

Diana leaned wearily against the counter, battling a strong desire to see Ian and a strong desire not to. The nurse returned, telling Diana that she could go in for just a few minutes. Diana signaled to Chris, and he nodded his head reassuringly as he watched her disappear through the ICU doors.

Ian's eyes were closed. His face and head were a mass of bandages, and his broken body was encased in casts and countless tubes. The heart monitor's beeps were the only sound in the sterile room. Diana stood close to the bed. Gently she touched his forehead and leaned over.

Her heart pounded as she said softly, "Ian?"

His eyelids moved momentarily...then there was nothing.

"You've got to live, Ian, you've got to live. It's Diana. Can you hear me?"

His bandaged right hand began to move slowly toward her, then reached out. She held it tenderly, afraid of hurting him.

"Di...ana?"

"Yes, it's me. I'm praying for you, Ian. Our Lord is with you."

His eyes began to open, and as he tried to focus upon her face a trace of a smile appeared. He kept whispering something which she could not understand.

When she brought her face close to his, she heard him say, "I knew you'd come."

His eyes closed again, and it seemed as if he were sleeping. The ICU nurse came over to Diana and told her she should leave. Tears that had formed now spilled over, and she returned to the waiting room and Chris's arms. He asked her how Ian was, and Diana shook her head, not knowing what to say.

A few minutes later a doctor appeared at the

nurses' station and discussed something with one of the nurses. Diana walked up to him, followed by Chris and Jessica, and asked what chances Ian had. After a moment's hesitation, the doctor stated there was only a 10 percent chance that he would live.

Chapter Sixteen

It had been a long vigil. Chris and Diana had managed to sleep very little as they waited for any news about Ian. They sat together on a couch, Diana's legs curled up and her head on Chris's shoulder. The hours seemed interminable and the slightest sound awakened them—their eyes going immediately to the doors of the ICU. Jessica was near them in an armchair, sleeping fitfully.

As dawn broke, the hospital came alive. Nurses appeared with trays of medicines and orderlies carried out their various assignments, but the ICU's activities had not stopped all night. Chris went to find coffee for them all, and Diana stretched her tired body.

Deep in thought, her head in her hands, Diana did not notice a man approaching her. He was in his forties, and his face wore an expression of kindness and concern. It was obvious that he was a person who cared for his fellowman and was anxious to help alleviate a person's anguish and fear.

"Miss Diana Lewis?"

Surprised, Diana looked up questioningly. "Yes?"

"I'm Paul Evans, the hospital chaplain, and I wonder if I could have a word with you."

"Of course." Diana welcomed the opportunity to talk with him.

"I understand that you're a friend of Ian Kingsley?" Diana nodded. "I wanted to share with you something Ian said to me the night he was admitted."

"You mean he was able to talk with you?"

"For just a few minutes he seemed to be lucid, then he went into a coma and has been drifting in and out of consciousness ever since." Diana invited the chaplain to sit down.

He continued, "Ian was in great pain, but he seemed anxious to speak with me. I prayed with him and told him that he was in God's hands and that he should put all his trust in our Lord's love and grace. Sometimes these words seem inadequate when a person has undergone such trauma, but he seemed to understand and said, 'Diana believes that too. I've tried...but somehow I...,' then he drifted into unconsciousness."

"Thank you for telling me this," Diana said in a low voice. "He managed to say a few words to me last night, and I've been praying ever since that God would keep him alive." Diana faltered, then went on. "His experiences in Vietnam seemed to make it difficult for him to accept the fact that God loves him, and I've never been able to help him understand."

The minister touched Diana's arm and said, "Sometimes God has to speak to us in ways we would never choose, to get our attention."

"Yes, I've taken Him for granted for so long, and only two days ago—" Turning her face away, she said quietly, "I prayed that I might love our Lord completely. I gave this life of mine over to Him." Tears ran down Diana's face unashamedly. "Perhaps if I had done that sooner, I could have helped Ian."

"You sowed a seed; now let God nurture it, Diana."

"I know I have to trust Him, Reverend Evans. I suppose I'm still learning, even though I've known *about* Him for years."

"We all keep on learning, Diana, but now that Jesus Christ is in your heart, His love and grace will give you all the strength you will ever need to face the anxiety of times like these."

Chris returned with the coffee and offered a cup to the chaplain, who took it gratefully. Diana introduced Chris to him. There was a slight moment of embarrassment as she explained what had happened—that now she was going to marry Chris. Looking over at Jessica, Diana whispered, "She loves Ian and has for a long time." Diana's hurt and jealousy were disappearing, for she remembered the love and forgiveness she had experienced at St. Bartholomew's. Diana saw Jessica in a new way—as someone who needed that love as much as she herself had needed it.

"Reverend Evans, I really do believe that Ian will recover if we trust God."

He smiled at her. "Diana, there is no greater power in the world than that of God's love. Let's ask Him for His perfect will in all of this."

The chaplain left them, and they felt stronger for their visit with him. Diana and Chris were able to comfort Jessica when she awakened. She became almost hysterical, but gradually calmed down enough for Diana to persuade her to go home, assuring that they would call her the instant they heard anything. Jessica was reluctant to leave, but she needed the rest and a change of clothes, so she finally agreed.

They walked her to the elevator, and Diana hugged Jessica before she left.

"You look as if you could use a few hours of uninterrupted sleep yourself, Diana," Chris said with concern in his voice.

"I just want to stay here—at least for a few more hours." Diana looked in Chris's eyes and whispered, "Thank you for understanding and caring." She kissed his cheek. "You know how much I love you. There aren't too many men who would be as patient as you have been."

"Darling Diana, I know this is a very painful experience for you." He brushed a few strands of hair back from her forehead and said thoughtfully, "Hospitals make you realize even more what is really important in life—those you love. Nothing else could ever mean anything to me if I didn't have you."

"Except Him," she whispered, eyes turned upward. Chris nodded and held her close.

The doors to the ICU swung open and the doctor came toward them with a weary smile on his face. "He's conscious and we're cautiously optimistic of his recovery at this point..."

Diana was overjoyed. "Does this mean he'll be able to walk and lead a normal life?"

"It's a little too early to say, but he's a tough fighter, and with therapy I believe that he will. There was a turning point about an hour ago, and now all his vital signs are good." The doctor smiled again. "I believe this is going to be one of those cases that make us doctors know it's all worthwhile. You can see him for a few minutes if you like."

Diana asked Chris to call Jessica. "She probably hasn't reached home yet, but I'll keep trying," he said.

Diana walked to the ICU doors with a feeling of thanksgiving. Ian and she had been so close, and she wanted him to be happy and well. She knew it would always concern her if he did not find the same happiness that she had with Chris.

"Hi," he whispered weakly.

"Hi. Do you know how we've all been hurting inside because of you?" Diana said jokingly.

"If it's anything like my insides, I'm really sorry."

'Oh, Ian, I'm so thankful you're going to make it. I've been praying that you would." Diana touched his hand. "You know I'll always love you in a special way, don't you?"

He nodded. "The same goes for me, Diana.

We've had a wonderful relationship." A troubled look came over his face as he remembered Jessica. "I have something to tell you..."

"I already know, Ian. Jessica told me. I've got something to tell you, too. Chris asked me to marry him and I've said yes."

There was a long silence and then Ian said, "I'm happy for you, Diana. Part of me, I guess, was still hoping we would get back together, but it wasn't meant to be."

Diana bent over and kissed him on the cheek. "No, but we'll have the memory of some wonderful times." Finding it hard to express, she said, "Jessica...she'll make you happy, I know."

"Yes. We've got a lot in common. I love her, but in a very different way, Diana."

The nurse signaled that it was time to leave. "Got to go now, Ian, but you'll be in my thoughts and prayers. Get well soon."

She kissed him again and he whispered, "God bless you, Diana."

"You too."

As Diana reached the doors, she turned and in a loud whisper said, "Make Jessica an honest woman soon, do you hear?"

Ian nodded and smiled. "I will."

When Diana returned to Chris, he saw a contented smile on her face. "He's really going to make it, Chris. God is answering our prayers."

"That's wonderful, Diana. I left a message for Jessica with her answering service."

Diana began to gather up her things.

"Now we have something that demands our immediate attention," Chris said forcefully.

Diana turned wearily. "Whatever is it?"

Chris walked toward her and put his arms around her. "We have a wedding to plan!" Diana laughed and put her head on his shoulder. The joy she had known in New York with him was returning.

Chapter Seventeen

The English countryside was covered in a thin blanket of snow as Chris drove Diana back to the castle from the airport. She sat as closely as she could to him—it had been three long months since he had left Los Angeles for home, and their parting had made her even more in love, if that were possible. Telephone calls, letters, and airmailed gifts had helped to ease the long days without him, but now they were together again.

Chris took his eyes off the road for a split second and looked at her. "Do you know you're even more beautiful than the last time I saw you, darling?"

She leaned over and kissed him. "They say love is blind, but that's all right with me. Just always think that, even when I am 92 and you're tired of me."

"Never, my love, will I tire of you." He thought for a moment and said, "Do you realize that I've hardly been out at night since we were in Los Angeles together? That is some kind of record when a man of my past reputation is content to stay at home. Father has been delighted. He has talked my ear off about the castle. Since we opened it to the public, there have been so many details to take care of. I know he'll want to talk to you about it all—*and* offer you a job!"

"I'll love it. Is the attendance good?"

"Yes, and it's growing rapidly. We have a few minor crises each day, but nothing we can't handle," Chris laughed. "Last week one of your countrymen—an eight-year-old, to be precise—decided he wanted to see what it was like to wear a suit of armor. He knocked one over in the Great Hall and the noise was deafening! Then he got his head stuck in the helmet and it took us over half an hour to release him."

Diana laughed. "I hope nothing like that happens at the wedding. Is your mother exhausted from all the arrangements?"

"Sort of, but she's loving every moment of it. 'A Christmas wedding is so perfect,' she keeps saying, and of course it is."

Chris reached out for her hand and pulled over to the side of the road. A truck that had been traveling too close shot by, the driver yelling something indistinguishable.

Diana was laughing so much that she did not see Chris pull a small blue velvet box out of his pocket. "Got this at the same little place I purchased your bracelet."

Diana opened the box and gasped. It was the most beautiful ring...a marquise diamond in a glorious antique gold setting. "Oh, Chris, it's beautiful!" He placed it on the third finger of her left hand and said quietly, "I love you, Diana." She threw her arms around him and said, "I love *you,* Chris. Thank you for making me so happy."

"Happy? You don't know how *I* feel. Having you with me again, well, for once I'm speechless." He kissed her and they clung together, the nearness seeming to envelop them. Diana felt that if she were any happier her heart would burst.

Chris started the car and they continued their

journey to the castle. She sat looking at the ring and the gold bracelet that he had given her several months before. They were absolutely beautiful together, she thought. The ring fit perfectly but seemed enormous on her finger. "How will I ever be able to use this hand normally again? I'll always be conscious of this gorgeous ring." She pretended to greet someone, waving her hand in an elaborate gesture.

Chris laughed. "Do you *really* like it?"

"I love it," Diana exclaimed.

She put her head on his shoulder, still looking at the ring. As they turned down the country lane that would bring them to Castle Drayton, she said, "I know I'm dreaming...I know I'm going to wake up and be at my desk in Los Angeles."

Chris kissed the top of her head. "Not a chance. I'm not going to let you out of my sight."

A tour bus was ahead of them, filled with visitors to the castle. It turned in at the great wrought-iron gates, and Chris had to wait patiently for the bus to gather speed as it lumbered up the long driveway.

Diana saw the castle rising on the hill and remembered the first time she had seen it. She had loved it then, but now it would be home for her. It was hard to believe.

Some of the passengers at the back of the bus had recognized Chris, becoming excited and nudging each other and waving. He tooted the horn in greeting, which made the rest of the passengers eager to see who it was. The bus driver was extremely nervous, afraid the bus would overturn.

Chris drove over the drawbridge to the main entrance to the castle. Lady Drayton was waiting to greet them.

"Diana, my dear Diana. Welcome home!" She embraced her and they kissed. Diana felt very much as if she were coming home to her "family" at last. The earl also told her how much they had been looking forward to her return. He even had a tear in his eye as he watched his future daughter-in-law and his son, their arms around each other, go up the staircase to her room.

Chris opened the door and she exclaimed, "It's just as beautiful as I remember. Oh, Chris...I really feel as if I have come home." He kissed her and wiped away the tears that had begun to form.

Remembering something, he said, "Come with me quickly," and he rushed her out of the room, down the stairs, and across to the Great Dining Hall. There in an enormous pile were their wedding presents.

"Oh, Chris, we have been so blessed having each other and so many nice things. Let's reaffirm our vows from St. Bartholomew's and declare Christ as Lord of our new life together."

As they faced each other, holding the other's hands, Chris and Diana each expressed a prayer of thankfulness and their desire for His divine guidance. With the "Amen," they hugged.

"I forgot to tell you, Chris, that James will be flying over tomorrow night. The limited run of his play ends tonight, so he will have a few days here before flying back to start rehearsals for a TV series."

"That's great. He really does approve of me now, doesn't he?"

"Oh, yes, very much so. Speaking of approval, what about your sister?"

"Margaret? She's coming around."

At dinner that night Diana was very conscious of Margaret watching her every move. "If I pick up the wrong fork I'll probably be banished to the tower," Diana thought amusedly.

Later Chris took her to the library and played the Rachmaninoff record they had listened to over and over again when she had stayed before. "It's almost worn out—I played it every night we were apart!"

He looked at the bracelet he had bought her, shining on her wrist by the light of the fire. Turning over the locket, he read the inscription: To Diana—Forever, Chris."

Taking her in his arms, he said, "Forever, Diana."

"Forever," she whispered as they kissed.

★　　★　　★

The castle was resplendent with its Christmas decorations and all the preparations for the wedding. Diana awakened early on her wedding day, conscious of a growing excitement within her. She threw back the bedclothes, ran to the large armoire, and brought out her wedding dress, laying it across the quilt of the great four-poster bed.

It was breathtakingly lovely. She had hired a dress designer she knew in Los Angeles to make it and the result had surpassed her dreams. She ran her fingers over the fine lace and once more imagined herself walking down the aisle of the magnificent chapel. A knock at the door made her run for her pink silk robe.

"If it's Chris, you can't come in," she called.

"It's James."

Diana ran to open the door, and he swept her up in a bear hug. They sat laughing and sharing their feelings together.

"Diana, I really am thankful you're so happy. The Drayton family is *great*. It seems as if I'm part of their family already."

"You are, James. I'm so very fortunate—I feel as if I have parents again. I know that's what Earl and Lady Drayton want to be to me—and you."

Another knock at the door and the maid came

in with Diana's breakfast, so that she would not see Chris before the wedding.

"Would you like me to bring yours up here, sir?" the maid asked.

"That would be nice. Yes, thank you." After the maid left, James teased Diana. "My little sister, who used to burn my toast, now will have all the help she will ever need."

★   ★   ★

The morning went by quickly, and it was time for Diana to dress for the wedding. Her roommate, Sarah, had flown over with Diana's editor, Tom Bartlett. Sarah was to be Diana's attendant, but Diana had made Sarah go to her room—the excitement was all too much for her. Just thinking about all the aristocracy that would be at the wedding had made Sarah a complete wreck. Diana had told her to rest, and that she would see her later in the chapel.

Diana swept her hair up into an Edwardian knot, leaving a few strands escaping on each side of her face. The maid helped her into her bridal gown and smiled.

"It's the most beautiful dress I've ever seen, miss."

"Thank you," said Diana, delighted as she saw the way the exquisite lace accentuated her waist, then swept into a glorious skirt and train. The

maid put the bridal cap in place and fanned out
the fine veil so that it cascaded into a cloud
floating behind her.

There was a knock at the door and Lady Drayton came in.

"How beautiful you look, Diana! Chris will be
absolutely speechless when he sees you!"

She hugged Diana, then presented her with a
gift. "They are a family heirloom, and I wanted
you to wear them today."

The gift was a brilliant pair of early-nineteenth
century diamond earrings. They were the perfect
finishing touch to Diana's magnificent bridal
gown. Lovingly she looked at Lady Drayton. "I
don't know how to begin to thank you..."

"Diana, it is *you* I want to thank for bringing
to Chris the happiness that I have prayed for ever
since he was a little boy."

Lady Drayton kissed her again, then left, saying that she wanted to make sure the organist had
begun to play in the chapel. James arrived to take
Diana down, and the joyous reality of her wedding began to surge inside her. She was nervous,
yet her joy superceded any feelings that could mar
this beautiful day.

The maid handed Diana her bouquet of white
roses, gardenias, freesias, and lilies of the valley.
On her brother's admiring arm she walked down
the staircase, her train sweeping behind her.

Diana and James walked through the cobble-
stone courtyard that led to the chapel. A notice
outside the massive doors read, "The Chapel Is
Closed to the Public Today Because of a Private
Ceremony." Diana could hear the organ's glorious sound as the choir began to sing Sir Hubert
Parry's anthem, "I Was Glad..." Diana's heart
was pounding.

Inside the great doors was Aunt Janet, waiting
to give Diana's dress and veil the finishing
touches. They kissed and Aunt Janet whispered,
"You're lovely, Diana, lovely."

"I owe it all to you, Aunt Janet. If you hadn't
given that dinner party I wouldn't be here today."

It was then that she saw Chris waiting for her
by the altar. His handsome face was just beam-
ing as he saw his beautiful bride begin to walk
toward him. Her veil seemed to float like a fine
mist and her train made just the slightest sound
on the marble floor of the chapel.

Diana smiled radiantly as she passed the people seated in the pews, some of them familiar
faces. She hardly recognized Tom Bartlett, his
face smiling and his hair neatly combed. As she
passed the Earl and Countess of Drayton they
both gave reassuring smiles, and even the Lady
Margaret nodded her head in approval, seeming
to finally accept her future sister-in-law.

As she reached Chris he put out his hand to her,

and they stood side by side at the magnificent altar. Diana handed her bouquet to Sarah, who seemed to have fully recovered.

Chris's hands tightened around Diana's and she felt strength coming from him.

The Bishop of Drayton stepped forward to begin the marriage ceremony.

"I understand you both have recently given your lives to Christ," he began.

"Yes," they said in unison.

"Do you vow before this congregation to make Him Lord of your lives, your marriage, and to also raise your future children in the admonition of the Lord?"

Gazing lovingly at each other, Chris and Diana boldly stated, "We do."

The bishop smiled and continued, "Dearly beloved, we are gathered here in the sight of God and in the presence of this congregation to join together this man and this woman...."

As the vows were repeated, Chris kept reassuringly squeezing Diana's hand. The finality and beauty of these words made tears come to her eyes as she looked at Chris.

Speaking with a firm and clear voice, she promised to love and cherish him "till death do us part." Chris's voice was equally firm when he vowed to love and cherish her. Then he placed the gold wedding band upon Diana's left hand.

As they knelt before the bishop he prayed for them. Then, as they joined their hands together he continued: "Whom God hath joined together, let no man put asunder.... I now pronounce you man and wife."

As they stood to their feet Chris lifted the veil from Diana's face and gently placed it over her hair. He bent down and kissed her, and the joy of their love seemed to flow to each other. The organist began to play "The King of Love My Shepherd Is." For a brief moment they smiled at each other. Diana had shared the special meaning of that hymn at St. Bartholomew's, and it had led them to being drawn closer to that other Love.

The bishop, with a note of joy in his voice, announced, "Ladies and gentlemen, may I present Lord and Lady Christopher Drayton!"